Best Wishes!

Michael Hart

VERNE'S POOL

Michael Hart

Bloomington, IN Milton Keynes, UK

authorHOUSE®

AuthorHouse™
1663 Liberty Drive, Suite 200
Bloomington, IN 47403
www.authorhouse.com
Phone: 1-800-839-8640

AuthorHouse™ UK Ltd.
500 Avebury Boulevard
Central Milton Keynes, MK9 2BE
www.authorhouse.co.uk
Phone: 08001974150

First published by AuthorHouse   2/23/2007

ISBN: 1-4259-6776-0   (e)
ISBN: 1-4259-4935-5   (sc)

Library of Congress Control Number: 2006908580

Printed in the United States of America
Bloomington, Indiana

This book is printed on acid-free paper.

This book is dedicated to my dear wife and friend Gloria, who by
her very presence reminds me each and every day
that dreams can come true.

ACKNOWLEDGEMENTS

It would be impossible to list all my family and friends who provided me with advice and encouragement during the writing of this book. They were all instrumental in keeping my dream alive and without their help my work would never have seen the light of day. To them I offer my heartfelt thank you.

I also want to acknowledge our dear children and grandchildren, who always bring a smile to my face and love to my heart.

•CHAPTER 1•

GATOR WAS HALF ASLEEP when my cell phone rang. Truth be told, we were both nodding off and were startled when the call came in. Early morning fishing was our ritual on an average of four days a week. I fish and Gator sleeps. The old boy is nearing eight years old and has yet to realize he is a dog. On this particular morning we were fishing on the Elk River about a mile above the Estill Springs Bridge. The Elk River feeds Tims Ford Lake which is one of Tennessee's best kept secrets. Life is not too fast-paced on the lake; nor is the glory of nature more evident anywhere else than in the fall of the year when you watch the sunrise across the beautiful trees and calm water.

I looked at my caller-id. "You woke up Gator" I advised my sweet wife as I answered her call. "He will expect an extra biscuit for breakfast when we get home!"

"Rick Cheatham, the last thing that dog needs is an extra biscuit, but that is another subject," she replied. "Sally just called worried and wanted to know if Johnny is fishing with you this morning? I didn't think he was going with you but I told her I would check. Sally woke up and doesn't know where he is."

1

From her tone of voice my wife seemed quite concerned.

Johnny and Sally are our best friends and were part of the reason that Mary and I moved to this area. Johnny and I have known each other since our combat days together in Vietnam and we have had a close relationship every since. Sally has never been an alarmist. For her to call Mary at five o'clock in the morning showed the extent of her concern.

"I'll give Sally a call to let her know Johnny isn't with me. He likely woke up early and went big bass fishing down at Verne's Pool. He is convinced that the mother of all bass hogs resides in those waters. In the meantime, sweetie, Gator and I will be home for breakfast in another hour or so. Don't forget Gator's biscuit!"

"Right!" I heard her say as she hung up.

My call to Sally was somewhat unsettling. She said Johnny had gone out fishing last night and she hadn't seen him since. His boat was still gone. She called us because she thought he might have gotten home late after she was asleep and then had woken up and gone back out fishing with me while she was still asleep this morning. It would have been nice if that was the case, but he certainly wasn't out fishing with Gator and me. Sally's greatest concern was that she hadn't gotten an answer when she called him on his cell phone. It was very unlike Johnny to stay out of contact with Sally.

I tried to downplay my concern when I told Sally I would cruise over toward their vicinity and look for Johnny on the lake. I elected to do so not only to comfort Sally, but also to set my mind at ease.

"Gator, breakfast will have to wait awhile," I informed my fishing buddy as I hung up on my call to Sally. I started the boat and turned downriver toward Verne's Pool.

The name Verne's Pool is Johnny's invention. It is actually a portion of the lake known as Maple Bend. Maple Bend was a hairpin turn in the Elk River before Tims Ford Lake was created. Near Maple Bend is the entrance to the branch of the lake that flows to the old Winchester Springs area. Johnny and Sally have a lakefront home in Winchester Springs.

Prior to the lake being developed by the Tennessee Valley Authority (TVA), Maple Bend Road ran from Highway 50 to the south, through the farmland in the Maple Bend valley to Highway 130 to the north. Highway 130 was originally part of the old Dixie Highway built in the early 1900s to run from Chicago to Florida. Many of the early farmers in the valley found work building that road. When the lake was developed in the 1960s, the whole Maple Bend valley was flooded and now rests under more than a hundred feet of water.

Johnny had nicknamed the Maple Bend area Verne's Pool a few months ago, after fishing on the lake two or three nights in a row. He claimed that on a couple of those fishing occasions in that area, he observed lights deep under the surface of the lake. At the time, he was reminded of the submarine Nautilus made famous in the Jules Verne's book *20,000 Leagues Under the Sea.* Thus he created an imaginary name for that part of the lake. He called it Verne's Pool. I once told him that a more appropriate name might be Daniel's Pool named after Jack Daniel, whose distillery was not far from us in Lynchburg, Tennessee. I laughingly implied that "Jack" may have accompanied Johnny on some of those Verne's Pool trips. Of course, Johnny always strongly denied that "Jack" had ever been his partner on any fishing expedition, and I knew that to be the truth. My friend was too safety conscious to ever drink more than one or two beers while out in a boat fishing.

•Chapter 2•

As Gator and I traveled down the lake following the old river channel, between mile markers twenty-seven and twenty-six we passed the site of the old Eastbrook Hotel and Spa. In the early 1900s it was one of the fanciest hotels in the area. At that time natural spring water was thought to provide a great amount of therapeutic value and be capable of curing or preventing many common ailments of that day. In the age before the cure for polio was discovered, people would travel great distances to the Eastbrook Hotel and Spa to relax and bathe in its natural spring waters. They would be transported by train to the Estill Springs Railroad Station and then were carried by horse carriages to the hotel. Much of the Eastbrook Hotel's former property went under water when the lake was developed, and we passed above it on our way downriver.

As we approached "Big Eddy" (mile marker eighteen), I became more alert in my search for Johnny. When he was out fishing alone he normally confined himself to the area between mile marker eighteen and the Mansford Road Bridge farther down the lake. I had helped him "plant" some "fish beds" in that span of the lake. He would gather old brush or Christmas trees, which attract fish, and use concrete blocks and rope to sink them in near shore locations. Only he and I and a few select other fishing partners knew where we had planted those beds. Gator also knew but, like the dog in the Bush's baked beans commercials, he wasn't talking.

I could remember the general locations of the beds but Johnny could locate them exactly using his prized possession—a handheld three-dimensional (Trilateration) Global Positioning System (GPS) device. He would establish the fish bed and determine its location using the GPS. He kept a file of all the locations on his computer and a hard copy printout of them on his boat. That way he could return to them when he desired.

Unlike me, Johnny had an engineering background and understood in detail how GPS devices work. He once tried to explain to me the relationships of the GPS satellites, overlapping spheres, intersecting points in a circle, digital code patterns, etc. Before he got past overlapping spheres my mind had wandered elsewhere. All I know is that he could sure find those fish beds using his GPS.

My search took Gator and me to most of the beds that I could remember the approximate locations of. Unfortunately, after a couple of hours of searching I couldn't find Johnny's boat at any of them. As I searched my concerns increased. Johnny was just too responsible not to keep Sally informed of his whereabouts.

By now dawn had broken and on a hunch or perhaps just in desperation I started searching around the few lake islands that exist in that area. Those islands are really hilltops that were on a higher elevation than the water level when the lake was created. They are relatively small and all are uninhabited. I started my island search by backtracking to the island near the Devils Step Campgrounds at mile marker twenty. A circle around that island produced negative results. I moved back down the lake to the two islands near Maple Bend. Again I found no sign of Johnny around the larger Maple Bend island. The result was quite different as I circled the smaller island.

•CHAPTER 3•

As we rounded the south side of the smaller island I spotted Johnny's fishing boat. It was easy to identify because it is the only red-and-white seventeen-foot Nitro brand dual console bass boat I've ever seen on the lake. It was equipped with a Hummingbird depth finder, foot-controlled trolling motor, front and back fishing chairs, rod box, and all the bells and whistles that could be imagined. The greatest problem I had as I approached his boat was that there was no sign of Johnny.

The boat was floating about ten feet from the shore of the island. It was facing outward with its stern nearest to the island. As I approached, the boat was rocking in the waves but appeared to be anchored. I thought that unusual because seldom had I ever seen Johnny anchor his boat. The few times that he had, he always anchored from the front of the boat and I could not see any anchor rope on the bow as I slowly moved toward it. But as I pulled alongside I saw an anchor rope in the back. I tied up to his boat and climbed aboard, somewhat apprehensive regarding what I would find. At that moment I did not realize the extent to which my concerns would be realized.

Everything on Johnny's boat appeared as if he had parked it in the slip at his dock. The only exceptions I initially observed were that the key was in the ignition and there was the trailing anchor rope off the stern. I found it strange that all his fishing poles were in the pole box and appeared to have been unused the night before. Yet there was bait in the small live well, which indicated that Johnny's intention was to fish. It was like he had gone fishing but changed his mind and anchored near the island.

By this time Gator had gotten curious and joined me on Johnny's boat. I thought that he was getting hungry, and much to his delight, he knew that Johnny always kept some dog biscuits on his boat to share with the dog that Johnny always called "his useless black friend from Labrador." I was wrong in regard to what drew Gator to Johnny's boat. Immediately after jumping into the boat, Gator went to the stern and began barking. It was not a protective bark, as if he was barking at a snake or another creature. It was more of a low-pitched bark that seemed to say, "Come here. I have found something." I joined Gator at the stern and my worst fears were confirmed! Looking along the anchor rope and below the surface of the water, I found my friend Johnny.

CHAPTER 4

WORDS CANNOT DESCRIBE MY feelings as I viewed my best friend's body in the water. My thoughts ran the gamut from puzzlement, to disbelief, to anger, and all emotions in between. *How could this have happened and why should it happen to such a gentle person as Johnny?*

My initial reaction was to get Johnny out of the water. He was floating about five feet below the surface with apparently his left leg entangled in the anchor rope. I dragged the rope upward until his body was on the surface of the water and then secured the rope to the nearest cleat on the side of the boat. It was a much harder task getting him out of the water, over the side, and into the boat. I knew I didn't have the strength required to lift him straight up and over, so I took a different approach that was a modification of something I had learned while white water rafting on the Ocoee River east of Chattanooga, Tennessee. Our guides had always taught us, if someone fell out of the raft we should grab the person's life jacket and fall backward, using our weight to leverage him or her into the raft. The one problem I had using that approach with Johnny was that he wasn't wearing the life vest he always wore when fishing. Without the life vest I had nothing to securely grasp, so I had to improvise. I removed my belt and ran it under his armpits and around his back. I could now hold each end of the belt and pull upward and back. I hooked his legs over the side of the boat and pulled. In that manner and after some struggle, I was able to get Johnny's body into the boat. In that early dawn on the lake as I looked into his ashen face, tears welled up in my eyes and my thoughts reflected back to the greater portion of our lives that we had known each other.

•CHAPTER 5•

JOHNNY HOLMES AND I first met as U.S. Army infantry second lieutenants in Vietnam. We were both assigned about the same time as platoon leaders in an infantry company. On any given day our unit's primary mission was to conduct search and destroy operations in War Zone C. At the time war zone C encompassed an area that ran from Saigon (now Ho Chi Minh City) north to Loc Nihn and Bu Dop near the Cambodian border. Our main north/south supply route that bisected War Zone C was Route 13, also more infamously known as "Thunder Road." We were young and it was our first taste of what combat was really like. Sure, we had been trained back in the States to do our duties, but no amount of training could prepare us for what jungle warfare against a determined and cunning enemy actually involved. In our early days together, Johnny and I were friendly to each other but our duties were so overwhelming that we had little time to really get acquainted. That all dramatically changed one day about seven kilometers outside the small village of An Loc.

Our infantry company was conducting a sweep from south to north through the jungle west of An Loc. Johnny's platoon mission was flank security to the left of the command group and I had the same responsibility on the right. On this particular day a large contingent of Viet Cong (VC) forces were positioned to the east of my platoon. After action reports indicated that we had unknowingly interrupted the flow of men and materials southward to the Saigon area in preparation for the VC's Tet Offensive. We did not detect their presence and they allowed us to pass directly into their field of fire. When my platoon passed in front of them the world came crashing down upon us. I turned my guys to face the VC and attempted to suppress the high volume of fire we were receiving from them. In the initial clash I was wounded, as was about half the platoon—either killed or wounded. In addition, rocket propelled grenades (RPGs) were fired into the company's command group and we lost our company commander as well as our artillery forward observer (FO). This immediately left us without a central command to coordinate the actions of the individual platoons, and the loss of the FO left us without a trained individual to call in indirect fire to support us. As I attempted to mount a defense with my remaining men, the situation could not have looked bleaker. Then again, the one factor I was not considering was how Johnny would react to our dilemma.

As soon as Johnny realized where the attack had originated, he turned his platoon toward our direction and moved them rapidly into the gaps in the hastily formed battle line I had established with my platoon. He also had the presence of mind, as he passed the fallen FO, to summon the FO's radio telephone operator (RTO) and bring him along to our position. At least we now still had contact with our artillery counterparts, who could hopefully provide us with some indirect fire support if we could advise them where it was needed. As Johnny was organizing his men, I instructed the RTO to request that an artillery air observer fly to our location to coordinate artillery fire support and helicopter gun ships as needed. From the sky the air observer would be in a better position to observe all elements engaged in the battle and provide close-in fire support when called on to do so. When Johnny reached me we discussed two alternatives. We could retreat from our position, but that would present the unacceptable situation of having to leave our dead behind. The other option was to take the offensive and attack the VC in order to drive them back. We chose the latter. I will never forget how the battle turned in our favor at that moment as Johnny yelled to our combined troops.

"Boys, it is just like an army medic said at the Battle of Bastogue in World War II, 'They've got us surrounded, the poor bastards.'" Johnny then directed, "Stand by your guns, guys; we can win this little scrap." And that is what we proceeded to do!

Following the battle in which the VC losses far outnumbered our own, Johnny and I were sent to the rear echelon base camp for treatment of the wounds we both received. While there, we entered into a friendship that spanned over thirty-five years.

After our tours in Vietnam and discharges from the army, we each took advantage of the GI Bill to secure our post graduate degrees. Johnny returned to the University of Tennessee at Knoxville for his masters degree in electrical and computer engineering, while I enrolled at the University of Virginia at Charlottesville for my Masters in Criminal Justice. With only about a six-hour drive time between our schools, we were able to visit each other on many more than one occasion. Those visits were memorable in a number of ways. The most memorable was the night that Johnny met Sally. I had arrived in Knoxville on a Friday night for a visit and Johnny advised me that a friend of his had arranged a double blind date for him and me on Saturday night.

"Blind dates are bad enough," I remember saying to Johnny, "but a double blind date is surely a recipe for disaster! How will we tell whose is whose?"

"Just go with the flow," was his laughing reply.

When Saturday night arrived, I found that I had been half right regarding the disaster potential. My date backed out. To this day I have never been able to figure out how Johnny knew it was my date who backed out if we didn't know whose date was whose in the first place. This, of course, left me high and dry in a town I was unfamiliar with, so I tagged along with Johnny and Sally, the gal who would eventually become his loving bride. From the moment I saw Johnny and Sally together I knew that something magical was taking place. I saw my strong-willed, rough-and-tumble friend melt like a bowl of ice cream right before my eyes. From that night forward, their love knew no bounds. They were married the day after Johnny graduated.

Johnny and Sally's marriage produced several indirect results. First of all, they introduced me to my beautiful wife Mary, and for that I will always be eternally grateful. Secondly, their union resulted in the birth of my two godchildren, Brett and Vicki. Both are great kids and to them Mary and I are their "Uncle Rick and Aunt Mary." Mary and I went on to have two daughters and a son of our own (Mandy, Phyllis, and Greg), of which we couldn't be prouder. All the kids have been successful in their own fields of endeavor.

Following college Johnny sought employment in the private sector and soon found work with a private contractor doing work for NASA. Initially his work took him to California. Subsequent promotions and assignments moved them to Houston, TX; Cape Canaveral, FL; and Huntsville, AL. Huntsville, AL is approximately sixty miles south of Tims Ford Lake. It was while in Huntsville that Johnny and Sally made the decision to build their retirement home on the lake. Their selection influenced Mary and me to do the same. The added benefit was that we could be close to our friends.

After college my employment took me down a different path than Johnny had followed. I was recruited by and decided to enter the government sector by joining the Central Intelligence Agency (CIA), initially as a specialized skills officer. Later I became a field operations officer. Over the years assignments took me to Europe, the Far East, and Central America. In Central America I participated in a joint drug interdiction task force with the Federal Bureau of Investigation (FBI). In those days I was shot at on more than an occasional basis and was tired of being away from home and family for the extended periods of time my job required. Because the mission with the CIA was international in nature, I saw no relief from my dilemma in sight. I loved the excitement and thrill of my job but as I grew older and had more responsibilities at home, I realized I was not quite as young as I used to be.

A firefight in the jungles of Guatemala on my forty-fifth birthday convinced me that a career change was due. Fortunately for me, my friends with the FBI came to my rescue with an offer to transfer to their branch of the federal service. My new assignment involved a minimal amount of international travel compared to my duties with the CIA. When I eventually retired, I was a deputy to the director who was responsible for the FBI field offices in sixteen States.

•Chapter 6•

My thoughts returned to the task at hand and what I had to do. I had never made a 911 call from my cell phone and had no idea where it might be routed. We have three-way calling service on our home phone, so I knew that if I called Mary she would be able to patch me through to the 911 dispatch center. Besides, I would need Mary's help when we told Sally what I had found. That was a task I tried to put out of my mind.

I called Mary.

"Hey sweetie, when are you and Gator coming home for breakfast?" Mary asked. "My two boys must be getting mighty hungry by now."

"Mary, I have something I need to tell you and I need your help," I replied. "I just don't know how to say what I have to tell you."

I heard the fright in her voice as she asked, "Are you and Gator okay?"

"Yes, hon, we are fine. It's Johnny; he's had what appears to have been an accident and is no longer with us."

The silence on the other end of the line told me what Mary did not have to say. Finally she responded.

"Rick, I am praying I misunderstood what you just said. Surely, Johnny is not dead."

"I wish with all my heart that was not the case but it is. I have gotten him into the boat but I need your help patching me through by telephone to the sheriff's department. Will you be able to do that for me?"

With tears in her voice she said she could help and in addition asked, "What about Sally? How will we tell her?"

"We need to talk to her in person—not over the phone. I will have to handle things out here before we talk to her. I think the best plan is for you to stand by at the house and wait for me to call and tell you I am on my way in the boat to her house. You can then drive over and meet me there."

"Should I try to call Father Bill so he can go with us?" Mary asked.

"That is an excellent idea. Please call him after we talk to the sheriff's office. Then again, what if she calls you before we head over to her house to see if I have found anything?" I asked.

"You have enough to worry about. I will think of something to tell her if she calls. I'll dial 911 now."

Mary dialed 911 and flashed the telephone switch hook to add me to the call.

After two rings the 911 operator answered. "Nine-one-one center. Is this call coming from the Cheatham residence?"

"Yes," I responded. "But I have been added by my wife to this call and I have an emergency situation on the lake that requires the sheriff's department."

She advised, "I am connecting you to the sheriff's dispatcher and I will stay on the line to determine the nature of the emergency and if additional resources will be required."

"Sheriff's office, how can we help you?"

"My name is Rick Cheatham. I am on Tims Ford Lake and my friend has drowned."

"Sir, are you positive he is dead?" was the immediate response to my statement.

"Yes, I am positive! I found him submerged in the water a few minutes ago and it appears he had been there for some time."

The sheriff's dispatcher advised me to hold for a moment while a deputy picked up the line.

"This is Deputy Reynolds. Is this Rick Cheatham on the line?"

I have known Tom Reynolds for some time through the Lions Club and that is why he recognized my name.

"Yes Tom, this is Rick. Johnny Holmes has drowned. Right now I am on the lake at the smaller island near Maple Bend. I have Johnny in the boat but it appears he has been dead for a while."

"Were you two fishing together?" Tom asked.

"No, he didn't come home last night and his wife Sally called Mary and me early this morning. I just found him a little while ago. Should I stay where I am at or bring his boat over to the Devils Step boat ramp and meet you all there? I have my boat tied up to his right now"

Tom advised that he was calling their chief investigator, Adam King, and would let me know what to do in just a minute.

When he came back on the line he told me to meet them at the Devils Step Ramp. He said that since the accident involved the lake, he was also contacting the Tennessee Wildlife Resources Agency which also has responsibility for incidences that take place on Tims Ford.

I replied, "Tom, I am sure this could go unsaid, but I'll advise anyway. Please, whatever you all do, do not contact his wife, Sally. There is nothing she can do right now. Mary is getting in contact with our rector and hopefully he will join Mary and me when we tell Sally what has happened. An impersonal call to her right now would be devastating."

Tom acknowledged my request with a firm, "You have my assurance we won't call her until we know you have talked to her. God bless you, I do not envy you and your wife that task."

Lastly I asked, "Are there any other questions before I start moving the boats?"

The multiple answers I received from everyone on the call were all "no."

With both boats lashed together I did not want to move at a very fast pace. When I was about halfway between the island and Devils Step landing, I heard the first sirens in the distance.

·CHAPTER 7·

As I ROUNDED A bend in the lake and came within sight of the Devils Step Public Boat Ramp I wished I had asked the Sheriff's Department not to use their sirens. In the quiet of the early morning I knew that sound can travel a great distance across the lake and I was concerned that Sally might hear the distant sirens at her house and become more alarmed than she already was.

As I approach the boat ramp, two sheriff's department cars were visible as well as an ambulance. All had their emergency lights on. I could see Tom Reynolds in his deputy uniform and another man in civilian clothes wrapping crime scene tape around the railing on the right side of the dock. I assumed the other person was Adam King and that was where they wanted me to tie up the boats. I eased in as close to the ramp end of the dock as I could, shut down my boat, and stepped out onto the concrete. Captain King greeted me and introduced himself.

"Mr. Cheatham, my name is Captain Adam King with the Franklin County Sheriff's Department. Our agency is assuming primary responsibility for this investigation and I will be the chief investigator into Mr. Holmes's death. First, let me extend my condolences to you for the loss of your friend. We will have a few questions to ask you and I will keep them as brief as possible because I realize the emotional turmoil you must be experiencing right now."

"I'll tell you what I know but my information is limited at best. As soon as you are finished with me, I will be joining my wife at Johnny and Sally's home so we can tell her what has happened to Johnny."

By this time another deputy had arrived to keep the early morning fishermen and folks from the nearby campground at a distance. That deputy freed up Tom Reynolds so he could join Captain King and me.

Tom shook my hand, put his other arm around my shoulder, and said, "Rick I don't know what to say except I am sorry about your friend. We will not bother you any more than absolutely necessary."

"Thanks, Tom," I replied.

Captain King then advised that an agent from the Tennessee Wildlife Resources Agency (TWRA) would be joining them as soon as one was located and could be notified. Among many other duties, TWRA is responsibility for boating safety on all public lakes in the state of Tennessee. It made sense that they would also be involved in the investigation and would have to report their findings through their lines of organization.

As a point of law, Captain King explained that the coroner would not be involved unless the death occurred as a result of criminal or other violent means, or in any other suspicious or unusual manner. He advised that in the past the coroner was not usually involved when death was caused by accidental drowning. Therefore, he didn't think the coroner would be called. He said he would reserve that decision until later, but it appeared from his tone of voice that he was already leaning in that direction.

By this time Ronnie Shutliff with the Tennessee Wildlife Resources Agency had arrived and I was introduced to him. Now that a representative of TWRA was on the scene, Captain King was able to proceed with his investigation. After filling out witness information regarding my full name, address, etc., Captain King proceeded to ask specific questions concerning what I had found.

"Mr. Cheatham, what caused you to start searching for Mr. Holmes early this morning?"

I explained Sally's call to Mary and how that call had resulted in my search.

"Can you estimate the time and tell us where you found him?" Captain King continued.

"I didn't look at my watch but I know it was around six o'clock when I found Johnny," I answered. "I could pinpoint on a map where his boat was. Generally I would say it was on the south side of the smallest island that is in the vicinity of Maple Bend."

"Under what conditions did you find his body?"

This question caused my mind to "rerun" the scene I had observed when I found Johnny, and I tried to clear my mind of emotion as best I could as I answered their question. Tom Reynolds seemed to feel the stress I was under while recalling these events because he retrieved the thermos of coffee from my boat and poured me a cup. The coffee helped and I explained to Captain King what I had found.

Captain King continued his questions by asking, "Did you observe anyone around or near the boat when you found it?"

"I saw no one else on the lake near us when I found him," I advised.

At this point Ronnie Shutliff with TWRA interjected a question. "Mr. Cheatham, you just said 'no one else was on the lake near us.' By 'us,' do you mean that someone else was in your boat with you?"

"No," I replied. "I didn't mean to mislead you. When I said 'us' I meant my dog Gator and me."

"Did you observe anything that would lead you to believe that any sort of violence was involved in Mr. Holmes's death?"

"Not really" was my answer. "It appears his foot became entangled in the anchor rope and he was pulled overboard and couldn't free himself."

"That is what it looks like to me," Captain King said. "But it is my job to explore all possibilities before forming a final opinion. I hope you understand."

"I understand! I have spent the greater part of my life in the CIA and FBI, so I am familiar with the paths you have to explore in your investigations. I just wish my buddy wasn't dead and, as a result, you wouldn't be asking me these questions."

"Forgive me for having to ask this, but Mr. Cheatham, did Johnny have any reason to possibly want to take his own life?"

A lump formed in my throat as I tried to answer. "I will say this. Johnny and Sally have what some refer to as a million-dollar family. They have been successful, their children have been successful, and they could not be prouder of their children. To my knowledge Johnny was in perfect health. Most of his aches and pains were self-inflected from the busy schedule he maintained. He loved retirement and attacked it with zeal. I don't believe the word *suicide* was in Johnny's vocabulary."

"For the record, Mr. Cheatham, is this how you found the boat? Has anything been added or removed?"

"I can't think of anything except my belt, which I used to help get him out of the water."

Captain King continued, "We have just one other task we need to perform here before the body is transported to the hospital. We need to inventory Mr. Holmes's valuables and the major contents of the boat. It would be most helpful to us if you could stay here while we do that. It shouldn't take but a few minutes."

I agreed to stay because I was most familiar with the contents for Johnny's boat. While they were preparing for the inventory, I advised Tom Reynolds that in a couple of hours they should be able to pick up the boat trailer at Sally's house so they could haul Johnny's boat to wherever they had to take it. I needed those two hours to give Mary and me time to break the news to Sally.

While I was waiting for them to begin the inventory, I noticed a look of puzzlement on Ronnie Shutliff's face as he looked around Johnny's boat. He then asked, "I don't see a life vest on Mr. Holmes's body or in his boat. Was he wearing one when he drowned?"

His question reminded me of one of my first observations when I had found Johnny: He wasn't wearing his life vest.

"Ronnie, that's a good point. Johnny was a pure-to-the-core University of Tennessee alumni and fan. He generally kept himself surrounded with UT's orange and white colors. He had a UT life vest he always wore when he was fishing. I don't know where it is now and I have no idea why he wasn't wearing it when I found him!"

Ronnie noted what I said on the TWRA report he was preparing. He then showed me a picture of examples of the different U.S. Coast Guard approved floatation devises and asked me to identify which type Johnny normally wore. My best guess was that it was a type III rated life vest.

By then the sheriff's department was ready to conduct the inventory and I joined them on the boat.

The first things they noted on their inventory sheet were the contents of Johnny's billfold and his jewelry. They noted that the billfold contained 186 dollars in cash and that he was wearing two rings: a gold wedding ring on his left hand and a ring with four diamonds on his right hand.

The contents of the boat came next. We listed his iPOD digital music player, four sets of fishing rods and reels, and a three-drawer tackle box. As I looked about more closely I realized his cell phone and GPS device were nowhere to be found. I mentioned that to Captain King.

"In all probability if he had them in his pockets, they were lost when he fell overboard," said Captain King.

"I guess I'm not terribly comfortable with that theory now that I reflect on things," I said. "Johnny had a custom leather holster for his GPS device made for him at a leather shop up in Lynchburg. You can see it there near the dashboard on the boat. That was where he kept the GPS when he was fishing. It doesn't seem reasonable to me that the GPS fell overboard—the cell phone maybe, but not the GPS."

Captain King didn't respond directly to my comments. All he did following the inventory was advise everyone, "I am going to instruct the ambulance crew to transport Mr. Holmes's body to the Southern Tennessee Medical Center in Winchester for certification of his death by a doctor. Based on the information I have so far, I do not believe our office will request a coroner's inquest or autopsy. The family will need to arrange with a funeral director to pick up his body from the hospital."

King then turned to me and continued. "Rick, I would appreciate if you could advise Mrs. Holmes that I will need to visit her in the next couple of days to ask her some routine questions. I wish that wasn't necessary but unfortunately it is. Tom will arrange to pick up the boat trailer so the boat can be loaded and taken to the compound at the sheriff's office. Until that is done we will keep the boat ramp closed. Are there any other questions before we close up here?"

"I just have a question on why there will be no coroner's inquest," I interjected. "I realize the sheriff's office can make the decision whether to request one or not and you are looking at this as an accidental drowning. Still, it seems to me that a couple of things don't line up and should require further consideration. Johnny was in the water with no life vest and his cell phone and GPS are missing. To me, that doesn't add up."

"Rick," Captain King said. "I can only imagine how depressing this is to you, and I truly respect your point of view. I also know that in situations such as this, those closest to the deceased are heavily influenced by the emotions of the moment. There is no apparent physical harm involved and I feel there is a logical explanation for the absence of the items you mentioned. If a robbery was involved, it would seem to me that his money, iPOD, and fishing gear would also be missing. Therefore, unless something else develops, I must stand behind my initial finding of accidental death. I hope you can understand my position."

"Let me say this. I understand what you are saying, but things just don't seem quite right to me. Maybe I'll look at things differently tomorrow. However, right now I can't see how his death can be wrapped up in such a neat little package."

Following our discussion I placed a call to Mary.

$\bullet$ CHAPTER 8 $\bullet$

WHEN MARY ANSWERED I asked, "Hon, how are you holding up?"

"About as well as can be expected. Father Bill is here and we have been waiting for your call. I am going to put him on the line."

Father Bill Midgett, his wife, and their beautiful family are about the finest thing that has happened to Trinity Church in Winchester, Tennessee in a number of years. Johnny and Sally attended there regularly and naturally took Mary and me there as guests when we first moved to the lake. The first visit sold us. We had never observed such a close-knit and friendly church family in all the locations where we had lived. It was also readily obvious that the *thread that held the cloth together* was the compassionate heart of Father Bill and his concern for the lives of each and every member of his congregation.

"Rick, we are so sorry about Johnny. I am sure you know that he has already joined our Father in heaven, and that his reward is well deserved. I am glad that you and Mary called me in this time of trial, and you know I will be here to do what I can and provide comfort for Sally and their family."

"Thank you Father Bill, it will be comforting to know you are with us when we tell Sally of her loss."

I made arrangements to meet Mary and Father Bill at Sally's house. From the hill on the road above the house they would be able to see me arrive in the boat and they could join me at that time. Gator and I then set out in the boat for Sally's house.

When I arrived and tied up the boat at the dock, I went to the front door, where Mary and Father Bill met me. As soon as the three of us stepped onto the porch, the front door opened and Sally met us with a look of fear in her eyes.

"Oh please God, don't tell me something has happened to my Johnny," Sally cried as Mary took her into her arms.

The four of us entered the house and Mary guided Sally to the couch.

My voice was breaking as I explained, "Sally, there has been an accident and Johnny is with his maker in heaven. We are so, so sorry to bring this news to you." At that point, Sally tried to speak but her words were lost in her cry of anguish.

Father Bill then spoke. "Sally, we understand the pain to you that this news brings. We can only take comfort that Johnny is in a better place. There was a great love the two of you shared and we know at this time your heart is breaking. Your whole church family shares your loss and we will be here now and in the future to help you and your family in this time of need. Perhaps we may find some peace in our heart as we look to the twenty-third psalm of David. The Lord is my Shepard; I shall not want…"

After Father Bill finished the twenty-third psalm and offered a brief prayer, I was at a loss for words. Mary spoke up first. "Sally, I will be here with you as long as you need me. There will be decisions that have to be made but we won't rush that. All will get done in due time. I think the most important thing at the moment is for Brett and Vicki to be contacted so they can make plans to get here as soon as possible. Do you want Rick and me to make those calls for you?"

"I love them so much and should be the one to call them," Sally replied. "But I am not sure I am up to it. If you or Rick could call them, it would help. Tell them I love them and need them more than ever right now."

"I will do that immediately," Mary said as she headed for the phone in the kitchen.

Sally sat in silence for a few minutes, then asked in a quivering voice, "Rick, what happened?"

I explained as best I could what apparently had happened without getting into any more detail than necessary. I avoided making her aware that, to an extent, I disagreed with Captain King's findings. I had to work things out in my own mind and there was no reason to burden Sally with my concerns.

"I will call the sheriff's office in a few minutes to tell them they can pick up the boat trailer. They need it to transport the boat to their office. When they release the boat I will pick it up and park it at our place for a while until you decide what you want to do with it."

"Rick, after you pick it up, please sell it for me. Fishing was so much a part of Johnny's life that I am afraid having it around will always remind me of today," Sally sobbed.

"Sally," Father Bill said. "I know in the past that you have been involved with some of the ladies in the church in providing help and support to others in a similar situation as you are now in. I speak for the church in saying that same support is available to you. Let Mary know how we can help and she will arrange it. I am also sure that Rick or I, or one of the other members, will be available to pick up Brett and Vicki at the airport."

After a short prayer, Father Bill and I touched base with Mary and then left.

In the driveway Father Bill asked, "Rick, where are their children now and how long do you think it will take for them to get here?"

"Their son's business is in Washington D.C. and Vicki is in L.A. I will guess that they should be here late tonight or early tomorrow morning. It depends on what flights they can get on short notice. Brett may be harder to contact than Vicki because he could be out of the country."

Father Bill's question caused me to pause and reflect back on Brett's and Vicki's lives.

After graduating from college Vicki joined a public relations firm in LA and has always been seemingly quite happy with her decision. From one viewpoint she is a close-to-home daddy's girl, but on the other hand, she also has a streak of independence in her. Her mom and dad recognized her independent streak early in her childhood and they encouraged it. They always felt that character traits, more than any other, would help her succeed in life. Based on her career so far, they were right.

Standing about six foot two with ruggedly handsome features, Brett was often described by his high school and college female friends as a hunk. I am aware of that because our daughter Mandy is two years younger than Brett. They were just buddies in their younger years, but about the time Mandy entered junior high all that changed. It seemed to me at the time that she had a crush on her "buddy." But what do fathers know? Especially when our children are in their teens.

Brett was always interested in the military. When it was time to enter college he applied for and was awarded a U.S. Army Reserve Officer Training Corp (ROTC) four-year scholarship and he excelled in the program. Upon graduation, when he was commissioned as a second lieutenant in the active army, he volunteered for and was accepted into the U.S Army ranger school at Fort Benning, Georgia. Brett wanted to be an airborne/ranger and was what Johnny and I referred to as gung ho.

To complete his ranger training Brett survived Camp Darby while at Fort Benning, climbed the 3166-foot Yonah Mountain, which is located in the Chattahoochee National Forest in northeast Georgia, and parachuted into Camp Rudder near Eglin AFB, FL for what he called his "swamp training." We could not have been prouder when Mary and I traveled with Johnny and Sally to see Brett be awarded his ranger tab at the ranger graduation ceremony held at Victory Pond on the Fort Benning complex.

For the majority of the remaining eight years that Johnny's son served in the army, he was assigned to the Third Battalion Seventy-Fifth Ranger Regiment. The Third Battalion has a proud history dating back to the

Sicilian invasion in World War II. Although he would politely change the subject if it was mentioned, during his duty with the Third Battalion, Brett was in Mogadishu, Somalia on October 3, 1993 during the battle that was made famous in Mark Bowden's bestseller *Black Hawk Down.*

After his discharge from the military, Brett formed a security firm in Washington, D.C. He recruited many of the comrades he had served with in the army, and they provide security consulting, site evaluation, and personal protection services for major corporations. According to an earlier conversation I had had with Johnny, Brett has also been retained as a contractor to assist "federal agencies" in providing security for visiting foreign dignitaries.

I had always looked forward to seeing our godchildren, but never in my wildest dreams did I think we would see them when attending the funeral of their father!

•CHAPTER 9•

THE DAYS PASSED BY me in a blur following Johnny's death. There were many things that had to be done and Sally was always foremost in our thoughts. Our oldest daughter Mandy lives about ten miles "up the road" from us in Tullahoma, Tennessee. Having her nearby proved to be a godsend to Mary and me, as well as to Mandy's "aunt Sally."

Four days after his death, Mandy, Mary, and I entered Trinity Church in Winchester, Tennessee for Johnny's visitation and funeral service.

Winchester, Tennessee is just a hop, skip, and jump away from where we live on the lake. One of the town's claims to fame is being the birthplace of Dinah Shore, and one of the town's main streets is named after her. Dinah had a TV talk show in the 1950s and 1960s and paved the way for entertainers like Oprah Winfrey today.

Two blocks southwest of Winchester's courthouse square stands Trinity Church, one of the oldest buildings in town. The church was established in 1859 and the original building was destroyed by fire during the Civil War. With its steeply pitched roof, tall and slender windows, and pointed arches, the current building is an example of gothic revival architecture inspired by the cathedrals and churches of Europe. It was consecrated in 1876 and is listed in the National Register of Historic Places.

As we entered through the door of the church, which we had done so many times in the past, I paused to look down the aisle to the stained glass windows above the alter and take in the beautiful colors painted by the sunlight pouring through them.

Visitation was scheduled to begin at ten o'clock and the service would start at twelve o'clock. Sally and the kids were already there.

Johnny's wish was to be cremated. Therefore, for the visitation his urn had been placed on a table in front of the alter railing and was surrounded with a picture and other items the family wanted displayed. His urn was draped with the American Flag.

In making their decision on what to display, the family chose items that reflected his life. The only picture present was one of Johnny with his whole family, because his family was his life. To the left of the picture was his favorite smoking pipe that he always had in hand. To the right of the picture was some of his assorted fishing lures; there to reflect the peace Johnny found when fishing and communing with nature. Also on the table was the Silver Star that he received for gallantry in action while serving his country in Vietnam. Behind the table the Christian flag was displayed, reflecting his deep faith in God.

Following visitation all items except Johnny's urn were removed from the table and Father Bill proceeded as celebrant of the service. During the service, two of Johnny's favorite hymns were sung. Then at the request of his daughter Vicki, Lee Greenwood's patriotic rendition of "God Bless The USA" was played to honor her dad's lifelong devotion to his country. We were sitting toward the front and I could only observe those surrounding me. Nevertheless, based on my limited observation, there is no doubt in my mind there was not a dry eye in the church after that song was played.

After the church portion of the service, everyone remained seated as the honor guard consisting of Veteran of Foreign Wars and American Legion members escorted Johnny's flag -draped urn from the church. They were followed by the family and friends who loved him in life and in death.

At the cemetery Father Bill conducted the graveside services. During the service the honor guard removed the American flag, folded it, and presented it to Sally with the words, "This flag is presented on behalf of a grateful nation and the United States Army as a token of appreciation for your loved one's honorable and faithful service. God bless you and this family, and God bless the United States of America."

Following the melancholy sound of taps being played by a lone bugler, the mourners were invited by the ladies of Trinity Church to join the family at the church's community building for refreshments and a celebration of Johnny's life.

Mary, Mandy, and I planned to join Sally and the kids at her house following the reception. We were little prepared for the scene that awaited us when we arrived there.

•Chapter 10•

A car from the funeral home took Sally and the kids to her house. We followed and turned into the driveway behind them. Brett stayed with his mother and sister up to the front door and then fell back to join us as we were getting out of the car.

"Uncle Rick and Aunt Mary, I know that mom apprec—" He was interrupted by his sister at the door.

"Brett, come here quick!" she screamed. "Someone has trashed the house."

My initial reaction was concern for Sally and Vicki because someone might still be in the house. Brett must have had the same thought, because he and I went through the front door at the same time.

"Brett, get you mother and sister out of the house! Put them in our car and drive up the street! Have Mary call nine-one-one on her cell phone!"

Brett's military training took over and he immediately responded to my directions without wasted comment. In the meantime, I grabbed the closest weapon I could lay my hands on—the revolver Johnny had always kept in the coat closet next to the front door—and began a search of the house.

I was fortunate Sally had not moved the revolver, but I should not have let my frayed emotions override common sense. I wanted to make sure the house was clear of any intruders. Yet in hindsight it didn't make sense to be wandering though a house with gun in-hand when sheriff deputies would be arriving at any time with the same goal. When a sheriff's car slid into the driveway and a loud speaker directed anyone in the house to come out with their hands up, it didn't take long for me to realize my hasty plan was ill conceived. I laid the gun down and shouted that I was coming out the front door.

When backup arrived, deputies searched the house and found no one. They then started their robbery investigation.

When Sally and the kids had arrived home, she had walked into the den to lay Johnny's flag on his desk. Upon entering the den she realized it was a total wreck. Files from file cabinets were scattered on the floor everywhere, desk drawers were pulled out, the computer terminal and cable modem wires had been cut, and the computer was missing.

Deputies found the basement door ajar and the doorframe splintered. Obviously that was the point of entry. Interestingly, that door opened from the lake into their downstairs recreation room, which houses their forty-two-inch plasma screen television, a surround sound system, and all the other miscellaneous gear that goes with it. An inspection of the rest of the house seemed to indicate that nothing else, including Sally's jewelry, had been disturbed. It was also puzzling that they would take the computer but not its associated monitor.

Everyone was upset. Vicki wondered out loud, "Why would anyone enter the house in broad daylight? How would they know no one would be at home." By asking those questions seemingly to herself, she arrived at her own answer. "Dad's funeral announcement! They knew when we would all be gone!"

That seemed to answer one piece of the puzzle, but the other question was, Why would they take a computer without a great resell value and leave more valuable "prizes"? Plus, what could possibly be in the files of a retired NASA engineer that would be of value to anyone?

With those questions still swimming in our minds, Brett and I retired to the basement to temporally repair the broken doorframe. It also allowed us some quiet time together to talk. We had not had that opportunity since he arrived home.

"Brett, this break-in doesn't make one lick of sense! Furthermore, I have not discussed this with your mom or your sister, but something about your father's death doesn't register with me." I then explained the same concerns I discussed with Captain King at Devils Step.

"Uncle Rick, my dad trusted your judgment more than anyone else in the world. Remember when I was fifteen and I was sure my parents didn't know anything? He came to you for advice. I didn't know he did until a couple of years ago when he and I bonded over a couple too many Bud Lights. He came to you then because he knew you would think things through before reaching a conclusion. I know you will do the same thing now. In the meantime," Brett said, "the computer is not a big problem. Dad has a memory stick around here somewhere with all the backup files on it."

"Are you talking about a backup hard drive?" I asked.

For the first time since he had arrived home, a smile brightened Brett's face. "Uncle Rick, technology is passing you by. For ages now, computers have had USB ports that allow the computer to communicate with different devises plugged into the port. The *computer gods* have now gone so far as to place bunches and bunches of memory—gigabytes—on little stick-like devices. Technically it is flash memory, but everyone calls them memory sticks. You plug the memory stick into the USB port and backup all your files. They are really great for moving many large files from one place to another. You download your files to it, hook it on your key ring, and then load the files into another computer somewhere else."

"Say again what you just said!" I exclaimed. "Just the last couple of sentences."

"You mean about the gigabytes and all that?"

"No! How do you move the files from one computer to another? I think you mentioned a key ring."

"Oh, the key ring. Memory sticks are little enough to hook onto a key ring so you don't lose them. Some even have a ring attached so you can use it for your key ring."

I thought back to yesterday when I had picked up Johnny's boat from the sheriff's office. "Brett, you've got to stay here with the girls for a few minutes! I'll be back in a half hour or so. I think I know where your dad kept his memory backup!"

I drove as quickly as I could to our house, changed clothes, and attached the service revolver I had carried while with the FBI to my belt. I still had my carry permit and under the circumstances felt it was the prudent thing to do. I then went to Johnny's boat, parked in back of our house, and set out to validate my suspicions.

I first checked to see if the key was in the ignition where I had seen it on the morning I found Johnny. It was there and hanging on the key ring was a device much like what Brett had described in our earlier conversation. Then on a hunch I looked into the compartment Johnny used as a map case. It was empty. That indicated to me what else I needed to know.

In the plastic map case Johnny had kept not only a map of the lake but he also kept a computer printout of the GPS locations he had mapped on the lake. My logic told me that if anyone was concerned about Johnny having recorded any one the GPS locations and found the computer printout, they would know that the information also resided on Johnny's computer. Thus, getting rid of the GPS and computer printout would not be enough to make sure the location or locations didn't get into anyone else's hands. They would have to dispose of the computer!

By connecting those dots in my mind, I was willing to bet the GPS locations file was the reason only the computer was taken in the robbery and not items of more value. Then again, theory was a long way from fact and I had no real facts to back up my theory. The best I could do was return to Sally's and talk to my godson Brett. I grabbed my laptop computer and headed for her house.

At Sally's I took Brett aside, showed him the memory stick, and shared my thoughts with him. He did not disagree with my theory but couldn't imagine why one GPS location would be so important as to cause his father's death. I agreed.

I made my position quite clear to him. "Brett, I didn't stay alive and you didn't stay alive in combat by trusting in coincidences! In other words, I do not believe lightning ever strikes twice in the same spot unless there is a cause. I plan to find *the lightning rod* that has caused these events to strike your family twice. It may take me a while, but rest assured I will succeed!"

"Uncle Rick, you know you will have one hundred and ten percent of my support; just tell me what I can do."

"I need time to do some research but you will be the first to know when I need your help or advice. Right now we need to get back to the girls and I'm sure you can show me how this memory stick works on my laptop."

"I tried scotch taping it to the back but that doesn't work, so I need a Nintendo wizard like you," I laughingly said as I smiled at him.

In two days Brett had an important client meeting in Washington that had been scheduled months previously. His mother insisted that he should return for it. He planned to leave the next day and would return for a few days in a week or so. This fit Vicki's schedule because she had carte blanche permission from her boss to stay as long as needed. It was agreed, therefore, that their time with their mother might not overlap, but one or the other would be with her most of the time during the next couple of weeks.

I added one non-negotiable stipulation—that no one would stay at Sally's that night. In addition, for the next two or three days thereafter, Mary and I would stay overnight with Sally and Vicki at Sally's house.

•C H A P T E R 11•

MY DAYS AFTER THE funeral were busy and filled with more questions than I had answers for. Brett and I had looked at the files on the memory stick and they appeared to be just as Brett thought: backup to all his parents' computer files. We reviewed all the files and none jumped out as more important than the rest. They were fairly routine and the type that would be found in most anyone's home computer. I needed a starting point and I kept going back to the GPS locations file. All the locations on that file were for Johnny's planted fish beds, except for the Verne's Pool location. It was the only one that was different. That led me to a decision. I felt I needed to at least attempt to try to see what Johnny had seen at Verne's Pool. I made plans for Gator and me to spend a night there in the boat. About eight o'clock on that first evening we set out, equipped with an ample supply of coffee, sandwiches, and dog treats.

We arrived at the location after dark and I shut down the motor. I knew that I couldn't lean over the side all night constantly staring down into the water, so I established a mental schedule. Every fifteen minutes I would lie down on the front deck and spend about two or three minutes looking into the water. If I saw nothing I would repeat the process fifteen minutes later.

The evening was cool and there was little boat traffic. One pontoon boat was apparently trolling for rockfish (striped bass commonly called stripers in the middle Tennessee area) and it passed us every hour and a half or so. Other than that, we pretty well had that part of the lake to ourselves.

Sometime after ten o'clock Gator was chasing rabbits in dreamland and I was wrapped up in my jacket to ward off the chill in the night air. I was starting to envy Gator for being able to peacefully sleep and I was thinking this wasn't the best idea I had had lately. With apparently nothing happening below the surface of the water, I justified my decision to call it quits after another half hour. My next look down changed my decision.

I was about half asleep as I peered down into Verne's Pool for my next to last time that night. That was when I saw what appeared to be lights deep down in the lake. I couldn't really say it was artificially produced light; but something was glowing deep in the water and the lights were moving.

I have experienced a lot of things in my life, but what I was seeing was maybe the strangest and most nerve rattling I have ever experienced. I can deal quite comfortably with the known. On the other hand, dealing with something that is unknown, which might be equated to a UFO story, late at night and alone on the lake, was spooky to say the least. I have always been able to rely on my ability to reason things through, but what I saw defied reason.

I watched as the lights moved slowly about and I tried to determine if there was a pattern in their movement. Initially I could detect none. About the time I thought I might be seeing a pattern, the lights went out and I thought I knew why. The pontoon boat that was trolling for fish was making a pass right above the location of the lights and near my boat. I suspected it scared away whatever was the source of the lights.

I stayed out another two hours but never saw the lights again. A little after midnight Gator and I called it quits and I headed home to ponder what I had seen—*apparently the same thing Johnny had observed on a few occasions before his death.*

•CHAPTER 12•

THE FOLLOWING DAY AFTER some rest, I still could not arrive at a logical explanation for what I had observed the night before. Thus, I decided my first approach toward solving the puzzle should be an attempt to determine what—other than the mysterious lights—was at the bottom of the lake. I choose the Franklin County library as my starting point. That proved to be a good decision.

I knew our library in Winchester had a room downstairs that housed historical documents from the local area. A couple of friends had told me the documents in that room had proved invaluable to them when they were doing research on their family tree. Not only were historic documents from Franklin County and the surrounding area available, but someone was generally there to help. Those helpers are volunteers who have knowledge of the area and, in most cases, know the best place to start looking. In my case, Mrs. Andrea Crenshaw took me under her wing and offered to help.

Out of politeness, I never asked Mrs. Crenshaw her age. But I estimated it to be a young seventy or eighty.

She explained that she was a third generation native of Franklin County and laughed when she told me, "Ninety percent of the documents in this room more than likely didn't exist yet when I was born."

I didn't explain to Mrs. Crenshaw much about why I was seeking the information I was after. I just told her I was doing some research and needed to find anything I could on what homes, farms, etc. existed in the Maple Bend Valley prior to the lake being created in the 1960s. I didn't think it would be useful to support my request with stories of observing strange lights on the lake bottom. Surely that would not have helped—unless of course she was a science fiction fan.

"Why don't we start with the map drawers first and see what we can find there," Mrs. Crenshaw said as she directed me toward a cabinet on the side of the room with wide, two-inch-high drawers. "We have road maps, topographical maps, grave maps, old insurance company maps, logging company maps from the 1800s, and maybe even maps drawn by Davy Crockett."

I was really beginning to like Mrs. Crenshaw's humor. "Davy Crockett had lived in Franklin County, Tennessee, and his wife Polly's gravesite was a few miles to the south of Winchester."

"He must have drawn them before his visit to the Alamo," I countered with a smile. I was also curious. "Why do you have grave maps?" I asked.

"I call them grave maps," she replied. "They are really old cemetery maps with gravesites identified by individual. Some are more detailed than others. Folks tracking their ancestors use them a lot. Some of those grave maps are really important because whole cemeteries were moved when they developed the lake. Bodies were dug up and reburied elsewhere so they wouldn't be underwater. TVA left farm buildings and such intact, but moved the graves. You had bodies being moved hither and yon—mighty hard to keep track of them without a map, don't you think?"

"What do you mean 'TVA left buildings intact'?" I asked.

"The only buildings they tore down were those that would be near the surface of the lake after the land was flooded. I guess the others deeper down wouldn't interfere with boats and so on, so they left them standing."

We got started with the first drawer and handled the maps gently because some of the maps had grown old and frayed over time. Many were drawn by the Army Corp of Engineers when the Arnold Engineering and Development Center (AEDC) was developed in Franklin and adjacent Coffee County back in the late 1940s and early 1950s. One particular Franklin County map dated in the 1950s covered the area I was seeking, though the map detail was not precise enough for what I needed.

"I bet we can find an early topographical map in the fourth drawer down that will be more detailed," Mrs. Crenshaw exclaimed. "Help me put these maps back in this drawer and then we can look there."

After putting away the maps from the first drawer, we opened the fourth drawer in the cabinet. As she had indicated, it was full of a bunch of topographical maps for locations in Franklin County and some locations outside the county. We continued our search with those maps.

Most topographical maps are produced by the United States Geographical Survey. I am familiar with how to read them as a result my military training and field time with the CIA and FBI. Each map is titled by giving a name to the particular quadrangle the map represents. We were looking at map titles associated with locations around Winchester.

A huge benefit of a topographical map is the ability to pinpoint locations by identifying specific grid (map) coordinates for a location. Grid coordinates are used by the military and have other commercial uses such as surveying. The whole world is divided into grids; each with its own identity. Numbered grid lines (north/south and east/west) separate each grid. Distances north and east from those grid lines identify locations within a particular grid. Those coordinates are also sometimes called V&H coordinates, representing vertical and horizontal coordinates on a map.

One advantage of having a grid coordinate for a location is that it enables a researcher to investigate property records, etc., to determine who owned a piece of property at a specific point in time. In my situation I could convert the data from Johnny's GPS device to a location at the bottom of the lake—if I could find a map to match the data to.

A topographical map also has an array of map symbols to denote roads, highways, caves, large buildings, and a whole bunch of things. They are symbols that show on the map to indicate anything you would see if you were physically standing there looking at the location. If I could find the right map, it would give me a mapped glimpse of what existed beneath the water before the lake was created.

We had just about been through all the maps in the drawer when Mrs. Crenshaw said, "Here is a Belvidere area map. I will bet you a dollar to a donut this is what you are looking for."

"I don't have a donut but I do have a dollar. If you're correct, I will use that dollar to take you to lunch."

"If I am right, I'll take you up on your offer. But be prepared; I may be little but I can eat more than a dollar's worth of food."

We looked at the map and she was right. It included a match of the GPS location to the grid coordinates. Now I had a starting point that existed on the ground prior to the lake development.

"Bless you for your help Mrs. Crenshaw. Before we go to lunch I need to make a copy of a portion of this map. Then after lunch I will take it to the courthouse and start examining records to find out who owned that property."

"If I can save you a trip to the courthouse, can I get a dessert with my lunch?" she asked.

"Sure! I'll splurge for a dessert. I didn't know you had those kinds of property records here at the library."

"The library doesn't, but I have them up here under all this gray hair," she said.

Mrs. Crenshaw took a ruler out of her desk drawer and returned to the map.

"Look closely here and you will see that the location you pointed out is at the corner where Maple Bend Road took a hard right turn. That may have been the old Marshall place."

I observed that the road had a lot of forty-five degree turns and mentioned it to Mrs. Crenshaw.

"That was not uncommon for old country roads. In fact, many are the same way today. The reason is that when the roads were first developed, they followed property lines. I think most measurements of property generally are based on a number of squares. An acre is around 43,000 square feet, a section of land is a square, a township is thirty-six sections.... Do you see my point? Every measurement is a square. Thus, when a road reached the end of one person's property, if it was going to turn, it had to be a right angle turn because the properties were square."

"You know, I have never thought about it, but Mary and I have some friends over in Shelbyville. The road to their house is an old country lane and it seems like it has right-angle turns every quarter-mile or so. Now that I recollect, those turns follow the property lines of the farms on that road. Most of the old farms on the road have stone fences. Mary loves those stone fences but I told her it would cost an arm and a leg to build one."

"Do you know how those stone fences came about?" Mrs. Crenshaw asked.

"No! But I bet you can tell me," I answered.

"In the old days, when farmers plowed their fields, they always encountered stones. When they did they would move it. Otherwise, they would encounter it the next time they plowed that field. Rather than move the stones to another spot in the field, they would carry them to the property line so they would be out of their way forever. They would stack the stones on the property line and that is how the stone fences evolved."

"So they eventually had a cleared field to plow? I asked.

"Not quite. Freezing and thawing of the ground pushes new stones to the surface and those stones also had to be moved. That resulted in continued growth of the fences. Some people believed that stones surfaced because they were *tugged by lunar gravity*. I suspect that theory was dreamed up by someone who had one too many shots of Jack Daniels."

She leaned back over the map as she murmured, "I better get back on track here."

Before measuring anything, she examined the graphic map scale that represents distance in miles, feet, and meters. She found the mile scale and then, using the ruler, measured the map distance in inches from the Broadview Church on Route 50 to the spot I had indicated on the map. After she computed the mileage, she announced in a convincing voice, "That it. It's the old Marshall Farm." Then as she grabbed her purse she said, "The Oasis would be fine for me. They have a great grilled tuna sandwich."

We drove to the Oasis and after we were seated for lunch and placed our order, Mrs. Crenshaw proceeded to tell me what she knew about the Marshall property.

"The oldest Marshall I knew was the Mr. Marshall that was a friend of my grandfather. When I was young we would sometimes see the Marshall family in town on Saturdays. He and Grandpa and other men would sit in front of the general store trading news and stories while the women did the shopping. When Mr. Marshall died he had several sons but the farm was only passed on to the oldest, which was the old world way of doing things back then. That oldest son was Ike Marshall."

"Am I to assume that Ike Marshall was your father's age?" I interjected.

"He was older as best I can remember," she replied.

"Did Ike still own it when TVA bought up all the land for the lake?"

Mrs. Crenshaw thought for a moment. "No, Ike was in an accident and died early in…I believe it was late 1950 or early 1951. I could check the exact date, but I know it was either right before or right after my youngest daughter was born, and she was born in December, 1950."

I was making notes on my dinner napkin to keep track of her story and by then had to ask the waitress for extra napkins. "Let me ask this," I said. "When Ike Marshall died, did the farm go to his children?"

Mrs. Crenshaw chuckled at my question. "That answer is sort of yes and no. He didn't give it to his only child, Claudia, who was—how can I say it—a real wild thing. After her mother died when she was young,

Ike spoiled her perhaps too much. When Claudia became a teenager she had no desire to live on the farm with her dad, so she ran away and got married without saying 'boo' or 'kiss my foot' to her dad."

"Ike Marshall never got over that. He would send money to Claudia to help raise the little girl she had, his granddaughter, but he never saw his daughter again. When he died, he gave everything to the granddaughter."

By now we had to order dessert and Mrs. Crenshaw convinced me that the Oasis key lime pie was great, so I ordered a slice and she did the same. "Did the granddaughter come back to live on the farm?" was my next question.

As she answered, I could sense the wheels spinning in her mind. "No! The granddaughter had her own life by then. I believe she was in Texas or Oklahoma from what I heard."

"Then who owned the farm when TVA bought up all the land in the late 1950s?" I asked.

"The German guy that worked for Ike bought it from the granddaughter when Ike died. Let's see. He bought it sometime in 1951and I just can't remember everything that happened after that. One thing I do know is that something happened to the German guy right before TVA bought the land for the lake. I believe this fine lunch has dulled my mind."

"Mrs. Crenshaw, I would never accuse you of having a dull mind. I bet using your mind has kept you looking as young as you do today," I said as we prepared to leave the restaurant.

"Young man, flattery will get you everywhere! Thank you for lunch and for that kind compliment. For your compliment I will give you the name of a person that probably can tell you what happened to the German guy. Do you know Tony G. in Tullahoma?"

"I know Tony G. I am not sure there is anyone in Franklin and Coffee Counties that doesn't know him."

After driving Mrs. Crenshaw back to the library and thanking her for all her help, I headed for the Elks Club in Tullahoma, where I was sure I would find Tony G.

•CHAPTER 13•

TULLAHOMA, TENNESSEE IS THE largest city in Coffee County, which is the county directly to the northwest of Franklin County. By and large, Tullahoma was a small agriculture town until World War II came along. Then everything changed. When the United States entered the war, the training of thousands of troops in a short period of time was required and sites for that training were hastily selected.

Up to that time Camp Peay was a small Tennessee National Guard training camp just outside of Tullahoma. When Camp Peay was selected by the army to be one of its training sites, the land mass it encompassed was expanded to 85,000 acres in Coffee and Franklin counties. Its name was changed to Camp Forrest and thousands of soldiers poured into those counties.

During World War II, Camp Forrest was not only responsible for the training of thousands of army troops, but it also became a prisoner of war camp for captured German, Japanese, and Italian prisoners. Because of the wartime drain on manpower, many of those same prisoners were given paid jobs at Camp Forrest and off base at different farms and industries in the surrounding area.

Tony Gladson, whom everyone refers to affectionately as "Tony G.," and his deceased older brother Frankie are legendary figures in the two-county region. As boys growing up in Tullahoma, the two brothers were inseparable. Those were the days before a cure was discovered for polio, and Frankie was confined to crutches and wheelchairs as a result of paralysis caused from catching the polio virus when he was young. That did not slow the two brothers down. Their father modified a wagon and it allowed Tony to take Frankie most everywhere he went. Tony always claimed that Frankie "got the smarts in the family" and he got the muscles. They worked well as a team, with Frankie thinking of ways to earn extra money and Tony implementing Frankie's ideas.

When war came Tony enlisted in the army and was trained nearby at Camp Forrest before being deployed overseas. His older brother Frankie could not join the service but contributed to the war effort as a civilian accountant working at Camp Forrest. During the war Tony was wounded. The wound took him out of combat but allowed him to continue to perform limited duties during his period of recuperation. The army reassigned him to Camp Forrest during that period. Now the brothers were back together again and the bond was never stronger.

As the war neared an end in Europe and victory over Japan appeared on the horizon, Frankie and Tony knew that their duties at Camp Forrest would be coming to a close. Frankie not only believed their service would no longer be required, but he also believed there was a great possibility Camp Forrest would be closed. He viewed that as an opportunity and once again presented an idea to his brother.

Frankie knew that if the army sold the buildings at Camp Forrest, although they were almost like nearly new, the two-story barracks would be auctioned for pennies on the dollar. He envisioned that there could be tremendous potential long-term earnings from buying the barracks at auction, moving the buildings to undeveloped land in the two-county area, and converting them to duplexes with an upstairs and downstairs unit in each duplex. Frankie felt they could secure the additional financing they would need for the project, but he was at a loss to determine how they would be able to move the buildings economically. That was where Tony shined.

Tony proposed that they could buy army surplus wrecked trucks, remove their axles, and construct "moving dollies for the buildings" from the parts.

The army did close Camp Forrest and auctioned the barracks for pennies on the dollar, as Frankie thought they would. The brothers bought many of the barracks and developed their duplexes. A few years later the air force reopened the old Camp Forrest as a research and development center and named it after General "Hap" Arnold of World War II fame. The base was named Arnold Air Force Base and housed the Arnold Engineering and Development Center (AEDC). The influx of workers for AEDC caused a new housing demand and the brothers were positioned to fill that need with their duplexes.

With that early success under their belts, they expanded into other areas of business. They bought a lumberyard and also started constructing new homes. Home construction led to opening a cement plant. After the lake was developed and TVA sold the shoreline properties, Frankie and Tony were represented at most of the auctions that took place and their land holdings grew.

Frankie died in the late 1980s, but not before he and Tony had become well-known and respected throughout Franklin and Coffee counties for their generous nature. They were always available to listen to an appeal for help. If an organization or individual needed funding for a worthwhile cause, Frankie and Tony stood at the front of the line to assist. Churches, community centers, the YMCA, and youth programs were just some of the programs they positively impacted.

When Frankie died, Tony G. turned their diversified business operations over to their family members. Following his retirement; Tony G. took up residence at the Tullahoma Elks Club almost daily in the afternoons. He was never much of a drinking man but he enjoys sitting at his favorite table and, as he says, shaking hands with Jack (Daniels) and meeting with friends who happen by. It is a virtual sure thing you can find him there on any given day, sharing stories and experiences from his eighty plus years.

When I entered the Elks Club I headed directly toward Tony's table.

As I was halfway across the room I heard, "Rick Cheatham, it is good to see you, and the answer to both your questions is yes," Tony exclaimed as he stood up to shake my hand.

"Tony, the feeling is mutual I'm sure, but I am puzzled. What questions was I going to ask you?"

Tony smiled that sly smile that endears him to everyone and said, "You were going to ask if I am doing well and if you could you buy me a drink. I believe the answer to both is yes."

Tony may move a little slower in his later years but his mind remains sharp.

I told him, "A drink will be a small investment for the information I am seeking. Andrea Crenshaw sends her regards and told me if anyone would have the information I am hunting for, it would be you."

Tony touched my glass with his and took a sip of his drink. "Andrea is a fine person. She came from good stock. Her father was a gentleman and a hard worker. His word was his bond."

"It's good you knew her father, because if you did you may have known the Marshalls. I'm trying to get a little information about what happened to the Marshall farm after Ike Marshall died. Did you know them?"

"Sure did! Old Mr. Marshall gave the farm to Ike when he died. Ike farmed it in the forties and until he was killed in the early fifties. It wasn't a large farm, but it met his needs," Tony said.

"Mrs. Crenshaw, Andrea, told me Ike left the farm to his granddaughter when he died but she didn't want it."

"That's right! As I recall his granddaughter married a young man she met in college in Texas; I believe his family was in Houston. She loved her granddad but hadn't had much of a life with her mother. I guess she was happy in Texas and there was nothing here for her to come back to."

"So Andrea said she sold it to a German guy?" I stated as Tony starred off into space.

I wasn't sure where Tony's mind was focused when he said, "You know, I was never partial to that man; him having been a prisoner of war and all. I still have a piece of shrapnel in my back that I carried back from the war and the doctors couldn't remove. One of his buddies may have put it there for all I know. Never did receive my Purple Heart from the army."

"Whoa Tony! You just completely lost me. Let me refresh our drinks so we are not interrupted when you explain to me how he was a POW."

When I got back to the table with our drinks, Tony continued. "Here is what happened. You know that AEDC used to be Camp Forrest back in World War II, don't you?"

"I believe it was an army training camp, wasn't it?" I replied.

"It was also a POW camp," said Tony.

"During the war, some of the POWs at Camp Forrest worked for local companies and on farms around here because guys like me were overseas and manpower was in short supply. Doesn't sound logical but that is the way it was. Helmut Miller was one of those POWs and he worked for Ike on the Marshall farm. When the war ended, Miller went back to wherever he came from in Germany. Then again, he must have liked it here better than there because he came back."

"In those days after the war, many Germans moved here, especially to support the rocket program down in Huntsville, Alabama, at the Redstone army arsenal. A lot of German technology was being used in that program. How Miller got back into the United States I don't know; but somehow he did. Are you following me so far?"

"I think I'm following you and I can bet what you are going to tell me next," I said.

"You're probably right," Tony went on. "When Miller came back, Ike still needed help because he had no sons. So Miller worked on the farm again. You'll notice I don't call Miller by his first name because I only reserve that for people I like. Anyway, after Ike died in his accident, Miller bought the farm from the granddaughter. An attorney in Winchester represented Ike's granddaughter at the closing. The word that spread around at the time was that Miller showed up in the attorney's conference room with cash for the closing. As the story goes, it was after bank closing time when all the papers had been signed, so the attorney sat up all night guarding the money until the bank opened in the morning. I never figured how he could accumulate all that money working for farmhand wages."

"That is strange," I interjected. "Did Miller have a family?"

"He didn't show up with a family and kept pretty much to himself after he was here. You weren't around then after the war, but things were different. German Americans were an accepted part of our culture, but Germans like Miller were different. We had fought them in Europe and I for one wasn't real receptive to having them move into our community; especially so soon after the war. Therefore, even if Miller was interested in finding a bride and raising a family, his options were extremely limited. Besides that, he wasn't the sharpest tack in the box."

"Why is that?"

"You know, Rick, I've always said that there is an excuse for being dumb, but not for being stupid," Tony said. "I could relate a lot of stories about his lack of farming ability and other things. But here is an example of being just plan stupid. The Marshall farm had a continuously flowing spring, with water as pure as any you will find in these parts. Ike's father piped the water to the house and even during the worst droughts, the water never stopped flowing. After Miller purchased the farm, he had the bright idea to build a cistern to catch rain water. I shouldn't complain, because my nephew made a bundle of money building it for him. But it was just a waste of money."

Tony was fired up now and I had no plans to stop him.

"The cistern is just one example. Right before that, he had a whole bunch of furniture hauled up all the way from Texas and, according to my nephew, who saw Miller's furniture when he was out there, it wasn't worth hauling across town much less up from Texas. Then the poor guys that drove it up from Texas got drunk and ran off the side of the mountain going up to Keith Springs. From what I heard, the truck was burned to a crisp."

I felt like I had taken too much of Tony's time but I was intrigued with Miller. "Do you have time for me to pick your brain with a couple more questions?" I asked.

"Rick, I didn't ask but I think I know why you're looking for this information. I suspect it has something to do with losing your friend. My best friend was my brother and I still miss him. So I have an idea what you are going through. If I stayed here until midnight answering your questions, it would be worth it if it helps you reach closure over the death of your friend."

"Thank you, Tony, but if we stayed here until midnight I would have to sleep on your couch for two reasons: I wouldn't be in shape to drive, and even if I was, Mary would have me locked out when I got home. Therefore, I think I'll hold it to two or three more questions."

"It is a wise man that knows his limits, and more importantly, the limits his wife can endure. What's your next question?"

"Do you know where Miller went after TVA bought the farmland for the lake?"

"He wasn't alive when they settled! I have no idea who TVA settled with, but it had to be a relative of Miller, because he died from a rattlesnake bite a few months before TVA bought the land. The poor foolish fellow tried to treat the bite himself and wasn't real successful. The bite resulted in internal bleeding, which led to heart failure. If I remember correctly, he died two or three days after the bite.

"Must not have had any rattlesnakes where he came from," Tony added.

"Here's my last question, I think. You and Mrs. Crenshaw both alluded to Ike Marshall dying in an accident. What kind of accident did he have?"

"He wasn't really much of a drinking man—and like my Daddy always reminded me—moonlight, motorcars, and moonshine doesn't mix well. He ran off the side of Maple Bend road, hit a tree, and was thrown out of his pickup. Evidently the truck rolled over him because his body was pretty well beat up. The paper indicated that alcohol was involved."

I pondered what Tony had just said and then made a comment without thinking. It was more like thinking out loud. "He died similar to the way the two guys died on Keith Springs Mountain—except his pickup didn't burn."

"You know," Tony said slowly, "That thought had never crossed my mind until you just mentioned it. Write down this name; he is someone you might want to talk to."

Tony gave me the name of Hal (Red) Nelson and told me he lived in Belvidere with his sister Rita. "He has long been retired, but he was a deputy who I think was around when those wrecks took place. Let me know what you find. I'm generally always here."

"Thank you, Tony. You have been a big help. Take care of yourself," I said as I got up and shook his hand.

CHAPTER 14

IN 1928, HERBERT HOOVER was elected President of the United States. In March, 1929, when he took office, the economy and the stock market had been on an upswing for a number of years —most would say for too many years without an adjustment. That adjustment came in dramatic fashion with the stock market crash on Black Thursday, October 24, 1929. The crash destroyed fortunes, caused widespread bank failures, manufacturing plant closures, and extremely high unemployment rates. "The Great Crash" of the stock market threw the country into the grip of "The Great Depression" and people lost hope.

When Franklin D. Roosevelt ran for President in 1932, he was elected by promising the American people a "new deal." In early 1933, after being sworn in as President, he immediately began implementing his plans to bring about an economic recovery in the nation. One of the many programs his administration developed to get people back to work was the Tennessee Valley Authority (TVA). In May, 1933, the TVA Act was passed by Congress, and thus, TVA came into being.

TVA authority encompasses the watershed area for the Tennessee River, including all or part of seven states. Prior to the establishment of TVA, the economy for that area was in very bad shape—worse than the nation as a whole. Soil for growing crops had been depleted by mismanagement, timber resources had been cut down with no replenishment plan, and electricity was virtually nonexistent in those mostly rural areas. Without a good and economical source for electricity, businesses and manufacturers could not be attracted to the area to create jobs. In addition, there was no management plan for the precious water resources. TVA was designed to turn that situation around and over the years they have been successful.

One of the means by which TVA controls water resources and generates electricity to better the quality of life and create jobs is building dams on the Tennessee River and other rivers within the Tennessee Valley. When a dam is planned, there also must be plans to contain the water held back by the dam. That results in the creation of reservoirs. Tims Ford Lake is one such reservoir created by the building of Tims Ford Dam.

In the 1950s, Tims Ford Dam on the Elk River was planned and construction was completed in the early 1960s. In order for the dam to be built, TVA had to exercise their power of imminent domain to buy thousands of acres of land that would be flooded when the project was completed.

It was obvious that the old Marshall farm, subsequently owned by Helmut Miller, had to be part of that land purchase. The question was, Since Mr. Miller died prior to the sale of the land to TVA, who owned the farm at the time of the sale? If I had that information and could talk to someone at TVA, it might give me a clue regarding the source of the mysterious lights.

My first attempt to secure the information was calling TVA headquarters in Knoxville, Tennessee. I have never been known for my patient nature, but that call taxed my patience beyond my admittedly short limits. I must have explained my request to what seemed like twenty people and ended up in a continuous loop of referrals from one individual to another. About every fourth person I talked to indicated that a Freedom of Information Act request might be required, but no one could tell me for sure.

Having reached a total state of frustration, I hung up and tried another source—the back door.

Ted Carlson was a TVA watershed team member for our lake long before we moved here. Since, according to Mary, I have always been the "impatient one" living under our roof, we made a decision during our house-planning phase that Mary would deal with TVA representatives, county building inspectors, etc. I must admit it was a wise decision. She dealt with Ted for TVA dock and setback permits when we were building the house. During those dealings and subsequent contacts over the years, he has become our good friend. Therefore, I called him to ask a favor.

"Ted, this is Rick Cheatham and I am calling for a favor from you if it's possible," I advised when he answered.

"I'll help if I can, but first of all how are Mary and the kids doing?" he asked.

"All are great and how about your family? I replied.

"As well as can be expected with two teenagers in the house, but I'm sure you know what that is like."

"The good news is, although you think you won't live through it, you will," I counseled.

He chuckled. "I've thought of freeze-drying them until they reach their twenties, but I guess I would be hauled off if I did that. Now, how might I help you?"

I gave Ted a brief overview on the situation as I knew it, explained that Miller died a few months before the land for the lake was purchased, and told him the information I was looking for. I also gave him a heads-up that I had called TVA headquarters and was unable to get any answers.

"Did you by chance talk to Chuck Bonner in the real estate department? He and I went to school together."

"I don't recall his name, but I spoke to a lot of people," I told him.

"Let me give him a call in a day or so and maybe he can help. Nothing guaranteed, understand, but I'll try," he promised.

"Ted, that would be great. Let me know if you find out anything, and say hi to your bride for us."

"Will do, and I'll call you back as soon as I hear back from Chuck."

My next call was to Red Nelson. After I explained why I wanted to visit with him, he was only too happy to oblige. He asked me to stop by after lunch and gave me directions to his house. I got the impression that he didn't get too many visitors.

•CHAPTER 15•

THE DIRECTIONS TO NELSON and his sister's place carried me south from Winchester on U.S. Highway 64 to the turnoff on the right at Old Salem/Lexie Road in Old Salem. The Old Salem/Lexie Road took me past Falls Mill (the oldest and only working grist mill in the county) toward the unincorporated community of Lexie. Their place was a few miles up and on the left.

The house was about a quarter-mile off the main road. As I turned into their drive, a pack of dogs appeared alongside the car and followed me to the house. There must have been eight dogs and all appeared friendly. At least I hoped they were friendly. As I got out of the car a tall, lean man with a weathered face came out the front door onto the porch.

"I guess you're wondering if any of those hounds bite, aren't you," he yelled.

"Well, the thought did cross my mind," I yelled back. "Do they?"

"About the only way you could get hurt by them is if one of them wags his tail too hard and hits you with it. Poorest excuses for watchdogs I've ever seen. Get out of the way, guys, and let this man come in."

I shook hands with Mr. Nelson on the porch and introduced myself. He had a curious but friendly smile on his face.

"Let me take you in to meet my older sister Rita. Both of our spouses passed away several years ago and, with the cost of living like it is, we decided our pensions would stretch further if we shared a home together. This was our folks' place but we added on to it. She needed a sewing and quilting room and I needed more room for my guns."

Their home exuded warmth and a coziness that was very relaxing. He led me into the kitchen and introduced me to his sister. "Rita, this here is Mr. Cheatham, the man who called and wanted to meet with me."

"Hi! Pleased to meet you. Forgive my appearance. I've been doing the washing and ironing today, and my hair is a mess. Hal didn't give me much warning we were going to have company."

"That is not a problem. It smells like you have been cooking also," I said as I breathed in the aroma of country cornbread.

"We had black-eyed peas and cornbread for lunch. It's Hal's favorite meal, which is a wonder, because we were practically raised on black-eyed peas when we were kids. You would think he would be tired of them by now," she said.

Mr. Nelson added. "We grew up poor. Black-eyed peas were called cow peas back then and were grown for cattle fodder, used to fatten the cattle for market. You didn't tell anyone you ate black-eyed peas because then everybody would know you were poor. But you know, when I reflect back on it, we were poor but we had all the essentials we needed."

"I have a friend that married a Cajun gal in Louisiana. She tells a similar story about crawfish. They didn't tell neighbors they ate crawfish when she was growing up for the same reason. The neighbors would know they were poor. Now crawfish is about umpteen dollars a pound and the most expensive thing on the menu in a fine restaurant. I wonder if those folks in the expensive restaurants realize they're poor?" I laughed.

Rita pointed to the living room and added, "Why don't you guys go into the living room to talk. I'll fix some sweet tea, if you drink tea, Mr. Cheatham?

"I sure do," I replied as I followed Mr. Nelson into the living room.

As he eased himself into a well-worn recliner, Mr. Nelson picked up a book from the end table. It looked to me like the journal my grandfather used to keep when he worked on the railroad. I remained quiet and Mr. Nelson began to speak.

"When I went to work for Sheriff Tate, one of the first things he taught me was that I should keep a journal of my activities as a deputy. He said I might only make a note or two on any given day, but keeping a journal would help refresh my mind if events came into question at a trial, with insurance investigators, etc. Rita wanted to throw them out years ago because they get in her way cleaning, but I kept them. Sometimes Rita is more like my dear departed wife than my sister," he mused.

"Were you around in the early 1950s when Ike Marshall had his accident?" I asked.

"That is not hard for me to remember. I was fairly new to the department and that was the first accident I covered where someone was killed. Let me look. I think it was in January, 1951," he said as he thumbed through the pages of the journal.

He reached one page and stopped. "Here it is. January 7, 1951."

"How did the accident happen?" I asked.

"January 7 was actually a Sunday. Ike wrecked his truck sometime the night before. He wasn't found until the family down the road was going to church Sunday morning. So he could have actually died either on Saturday night or early Sunday morning."

I realized that Mr. Nelson hadn't answered my specific question on how the accident happened. However, I didn't know if he had chosen to be evasive with his answer or if he had misunderstood my question. I tried asking it in a different way.

I said, "Tony G. seemed to think Ike's truck may have rolled over him," and left it at that, waiting to see what Mr. Nelson's follow-up might be.

"I am about sure it rolled over Ike. He was banged up pretty bad. It looked to me like half the bones in his body must have been broken. Cars and trucks didn't have seatbelts back in those days."

"He must have run off the road?" I commented.

"Yep, Maple Bend Road had more twists and turns than a snake in water. It was a gravel road, so we couldn't identify any skid marks. It looked like he drove right off the road on the turn before you got to the old abandoned Patterson place."

"Maybe he dodged a deer or something," I interjected.

"He could have," was all Mr. Nelson said.

"Was it icy or foggy out that night?"

"It wasn't icy out and that shouldn't have made much difference anyway on a gravel road. Weather wasn't foggy either," he said as he looked toward the kitchen. "Rita's late husband was Ike's cousin, so I have to kind of watch what I say, if you know what I mean," he said in a low voice. Then he added. "The weather wasn't foggy but Ike's mind may have been a little fogged up. We found an empty shine jar in the cab of the truck and Ike smelled like a distillery."

In the backcountry of Tennessee for years and years, shine—moonshine, white lightning, everclear, and other names assigned to it—was an old Southern tradition. It is rumored that Middle Tennessee moonshine was among the very best because the water used to make it usually came from pure springs or mountain brooks that were abundant in the area. The water was mixed with the right proportions of corn, yeast, sugar, and malt; then cooked and distilled to produce a mighty strong alcoholic beverage—sometimes as potent as 190 proof. (Pure alcohol is 200 proof.) Generally it was distributed in crock jugs or mason jars.

If Ike Marshall had partaken in too much moonshine on the night of his accident, it could explain why he might have run off the road.

"Was there anything else that could have caused the accident—a blown tire or anything like that?" I asked.

"Not that I recall. It was fairly cut and dry. Looked like he drank too much and went straight instead of turning. Truck hit a tree and went about fifteen feet down the embankment."

"Mr. Nelson, I have one last question on Ike if you don't mind. Did he have a drinking problem that you knew of?"

"The county only had a population of around 20,000 back in those days and that was the whole county. Most everyone around was related by blood or marriage or at least knew everyone else in these parts. I never met anyone that ever mentioned Ike having a drinking problem. Plus, Sheriff Tate knew everyone around here who sold moonshine. If Ike frequently drank, Sheriff Tate would have known it and he never mentioned anything like that to me. Do you want a refill for your sweet tea?"

"I would appreciate it. It's good—has a little bite to it," I said.

"That's the Sassafras Rita adds to it. She boils the root and adds a little of the water to the tea. Our mother taught her that. She said it would cure what ails you. Interestingly, Sassafras and Sarsaparilla roots are ingredients sometimes used to make root beer."

He made a trip to the kitchen and returned with full glasses of sweet tea. As he settled back into his chair, he took the lead in our conversation. "On the telephone you also mentioned the wreck on Keith Springs Mountain. I assisted on that wreck so I know a little about it."

"If it is okay with you, I'll let you tell me what you know about it and I'll interject questions as we go along."

"That is fine by me," he replied.

"First of all the date of that wreck is easy to recall. It was exactly one week before President Truman visited Franklin and Coffee counties to dedicate the Arnold Engineering and Development Center. Truman dedicated AEDC on June 25, 1951, so the wreck would have been on the night of June 18, 1951. According to my journal, that was a Monday night."

With that said, Mr. Nelson started reminiscing about having attended the AEDC dedication.

"Did you know that after he became President, Truman changed the Army Air Corp to the U.S. Air Force and made them a separate branch of the service, on the same level with the navy and army? He also promoted Hap Arnold to a five-star general of the air force and named

AEDC after Hap. I was a part of the security detail for the dedication and afterward the President shook my hand. That was a proud moment," Mr. Nelson reflected as he took another sip of tea.

"I remember one thing President Truman said in his speech that has more than come true today. He said, 'The scientists who work here will explore flight beyond the speed of sound.' I bet Truman didn't envision that they would also be involved in testing for flights to the moon and beyond."

I hated to interrupt Mr. Nelson's train of thought but I needed to bring him back to the subject at hand.

"I guess the Sheriff department's duties for the dedication took priority over the investigation of the accident," I interjected.

Mr. Nelson turned his attention back to the night of June 18, 1951.

"That accident took place on the old Rowe Gap Road that ran from Winchester to the top of Keith Springs Mountain. It is now designated State Highway 16, but in those days we just knew it as Rowe Gap Road. They widened and resurfaced the highway in the 1960s," he said. "When they did they straightened it out some. The truck went off a portion of the old road about a quarter mile this side of the top of the mountain. It was a couple of hours after someone called our office to report the accident before we were dispatched to the scene. That wasn't our fault. In early 1950 our cars were still equipped with old Philco AM dispatch-only one-way radios. Headquarters could talk to us but we couldn't talk to them. This was before the VHF police radios became popular. The reason we were late getting to the scene was because of the surrounding mountains. The mountains blocked the dispatch message and we didn't receive it for a couple of hours. It happened all the time with the old AM police radios."

"Tony G. mentioned that the truck burned and the guys had been drinking. Is that correct?" I asked.

"He's right. We had to let it cool down before we could remove what was left of the fellows in it. Their bodies were burned really badly. The Keith Springs volunteer fire department helped us bring the bodies up to the road. It was a steep drop-off where the truck landed."

"If they were burned so badly, how did you know they had been drinking?"

"We were never positive, but you can put two and two together and generally come up with four. If a truck traveling uphill runs off a mountain late at night in clear weather and the cab of the truck is full of empty mason jars, the logical conclusion is that drinking was involved. If they were going downhill maybe brake failure would have been a factor. But they were going uphill"

"I can't fault your logic on that," I told him. "Did you identify the two guys?"

"We were never able to. The truck had stolen license plates so we weren't able to trace it back to an owner. One of the firemen had a girlfriend at the time that lived on Maple Bend Road. He had seen the truck that weekend at the Marshall Farm, so we talked to the German man that had bought the farm. As I recall, he wasn't one bit helpful."

"You said the truck had stolen plates…" I said, hoping Mr. Nelson would expand on what he had said. He did.

"We didn't have a lot of time because the President's visit was coming up, but we did talk by telephone to a Texas Ranger in, I believe it was Brownsville, Texas. He was the one that told us the plates were stolen. The ranger told us that it was easy to bring anything across the border if you knew the right people and had a little cash to spread around. Remember, this was back in the fifties and I guess things were a little looser then. He said people would bring vehicles across the border illegally and then steal license plates for them in the Texas border towns. It's hard telling where the guys had come from. Any identification they might have had was burned in the fire."

"You said the German man wasn't helpful."

"Not one bit," Mr. Nelson stated. "He said he didn't know anything— that his family in Texas had arranged the delivery from down there. When we asked him for his family's telephone number and address so we could follow-up with them, he really clammed up. Told us they didn't have a phone and he had lost the address. Said he and his brother had work to do and that was that. We never got one iota of information from him."

"Tony G. didn't tell me that the German man, Miller I believe his name was, had a brother living with him," I said.

"You are right about the German's name. It was Miller, now that you mentioned it. I don't believe the guy he called his brother lived with him. I got the impression from the conversation with Miller that his brother was just visiting for a few days."

I didn't want to overstay my welcome but I had one other question for Mr. Nelson.

"Did the truck have any cargo in it when it burned?" I asked.

"It was as empty then as it is today --- what would be left of it," he replied as he finished his tea.

By then Rita had joined us in the living room and was seated on the couch.

What he said puzzled me and I asked, "Is the truck still there?"

"It was hard enough dragging the bodies up the side of the mountain to the road. It would have been extremely difficult to drag the truck up with wreckers. Plus the sheriff's department would have had to pay for that to be done and we didn't have much of a budget. Most of what funding we had in those days came from fines for tickets we generated. We didn't get much in the way of tax dollars. We even had to buy our own uniforms," he reflected.

"Can you describe again where that truck landed? I'd like see it."

Mr. Nelson gave me directions and I thanked them both for their time and hospitality. As I walked back through the pack of dogs toward my car and was about to drive off, Rita added one last bit of advice.

"If you try to find that truck, be darn careful of snakes. There are more copperhead snakes on Keith Springs Mountain than Carter has little liver pills," she advised.

I wasn't sure if Carter still made little liver pills, but I appreciated her warning about the snakes.

After I left their place, I figured I had just enough time to drive to exit 152 on Interstate Highway 24 and make a purchase at the Fireworks Superstore. Roundtrip it would take me about an hour and a half, and I was comfortable I would still be home in time for supper.

•Chapter 16•

The next morning I mulled over a few of the questions I had in my mind. What kept surfacing from my conversations with Tony G. and Mr. Nelson was the similarity between how Ike Marshall and the two fellows in the truck died. That caused me all the more to want to visit the site of the truck wreck on Keith Springs Mountain. I figured that after fifty years there would be little left of the truck. Nevertheless, I wanted to be able to visualize in my mind what had happened on that night back in 1951.

I was well equipped for my visit to the site of the wreck because my son Greg and I had spent many hours hiking and climbing at the Walls of Jericho (up on the mountain), and I had plenty of rope and other gear that might be required.

The Walls of Jericho has sometimes been called the Grand Canyon of the South and is visited by thousands of nature lovers every year. At one time it was home to Davy Crockett, who hunted and fished there. For many years the land remained undeveloped. Then in the 1940s a Texas oil man, Harry Lee Carter, bought 60,000 acres of land in Franklin County, Tennessee, and Jackson County, Alabama for a timber investment. Yet he never developed the land for commercial use. For years the land was open to the public for hiking, climbing, and camping. Then when Mr. Carter died in the late 1970s, the land was divided and closed to the public.

Since the time of Mr. Carter's death, and fortunately for the public, a nature conservation group has been able to purchase and preserve about 21,000 acres of the original 60,000 that Mr. Carter purchased. This tract on the Cumberland Plateau includes rivers, lakes, streams, mountains, caves, and a host of plants and animals that are unique to that area of Tennessee and Alabama. The namesake for the area, the Walls of Jericho, supposedly originated when a traveling preacher visited the area and came upon its 50-yard-wide limestone bowl at the bottom and looked up at 200-foot-tall cliffs on each side. As the story goes, he was so impressed that he assigned a biblical name to it and that name is still used today to describe this wonder of nature.

As I drove through Winchester and turned left on Route 16/Rowe Gap Road heading toward Keith Springs Mountain, I was reminded of the many times Greg and I had taken the same route headed toward the Walls of Jericho for a fun-filled father-and-son weekend.

Mr. Nelson had explained that the truck had gone off the old road and parts of that road no longer existed after the 1960s. He had also added that the truck landed at the base of a cliff. About a quarter-mile below the top of the mountain I spied on my left what looked like an old road. I turned down that road and quickly recognized it was more like an overgrown trail than a road. I soon reached a point where it was faster to get out of my pickup and continue on foot.

As I walked down the trail, I realized it had once been a main road. Most of it had been washed out and overgrown with trees over the years, but I was still able to find old asphalt paving in some spots. In those spots where I found it, the asphalt was crumbled and mostly washed away. Unfortunately, on my walk I observed no steep drop-offs such as the one Mr. Nelson had described and eventually the trail circled back to the main road. Thinking I had missed seeing a drop-off, I backtracked the way I had come but again found nothing by the time I arrived back at my pickup.

I was at a loss. This was surely part of the old road that had been abandoned but I couldn't find any landmarks that would point me to the spot where the wreck had occurred. Thinking that perhaps there was similar section of old highway closer to the top of the mountain, I got into my pickup and headed farther up. When I reached the summit without seeing another turn-off, I began to question Mr. Nelson's memory. Perhaps, after all these years, he was mistaken about the location. With that thought in mind, I turned around at the fire lookout tower at the top of the mountain and headed back down.

On the way back down I rounded a curve and saw what appeared to be another road off to my right. It was obvious why I had missed seeing it on the way up. My angle had caused it to be hidden. It appeared so quickly that I passed by it and had to pull off on the shoulder and back up before I could turn onto this other section of the old road.

After making my turn I found I could not drive much more than twenty-five feet from the main road before the ruts in the road stopped me from going farther. I stopped and planned on walking this route as I had done on the one earlier. When I exited the pickup I walked a few yards to my right and from that vantage point I had a beautiful view of the valley below. That was great but it didn't help in my search for the truck. I was hunting for a cliff and none were in sight as I looked down. I also found that the trail abruptly stopped where I stood.

I dejectedly walked back to the pickup and got my cell phone off the dash so I could call Mary to see if she wanted to meet me for an early lunch. As I flipped open my phone and started to call, I stopped and laughed at myself. I was parked next to what many would describe as a cliff. *Sometimes you can't see the forest because of the trees.* I got my binoculars and walked back to the spot where I had stood. Sure enough, as I peered down, a flash of sunlight reflected upward. A closer look through the trees told me I had found what I was seeking. I was looking down at a burned-out shell of an antique truck.

•CHAPTER 17•

I SURVEYED THE LOCATION of the truck as compared to where I stood in order to determine the best route I could take to reach it. It was resting in pine trees that spread out from the base of the cliff. I had already made a decision not to rappel alone down the face of the cliff. If rappelling was required, I would delay my attempt until an experienced climber could join me. On the other hand, my experience told me that rappelling would not be necessary. It appeared that I could skirt the cliff by descending at an angle from the side through trees growing there. I locked in to that approach and walked back to my pickup to get my ropes, helmet, harness, walking stick, and cell phone.

Before I had left home I made sure Mary knew approximately where I would be. We also agreed that if she didn't hear from me by four o'clock, she was to send a posse hunting for me.

My pickup was positioned perfectly for my needs. I secured my rope to the frame and started a slow, controlled decent; always moving at an angle toward the truck. As I descended through the trees, I envisioned this must have been the path they used to remove the bodies. It appeared to be the only practical way up or down to the wreck. I could also understand why the wreckage was left in place. It would have been a horrendous task to bring that truck up the side of the mountain from its resting place.

It took about fifteen minutes to reach the site. As I approach it I kept in the back of my mind Rita's warning to watch out for copperhead snakes. Copperheads are not normally aggressive unless provoked. But when accidentally stepped on, they will strike out and bite.

I unhooked from the rope and took a closer look at the truck. Time and hunters had not been kind to it. It must have rolled so many times that the cargo compartment behind the cab had been torn completely off and lay further down the hillside. The cab was leaning up against a tree at a forty-five degree angle; apparently where it had come to rest. There was no doubt, even after all the years, that fire had totally consumed the entire vehicle. It also looked like every hunter in the county at one time or another had used it for target practice, because every window and mirror had been shot out and the rusted body was full of bullet holes. When I reached the front of the truck, I saw the manufacturer's nameplate still visible above what was left of the front grille. When I saw it, fond memories of my youth flooded my mind.

When I was young I had a favorite uncle whose parents owned a farm. Uncle Jim had served with distinction in World War II and I learned later most of his time was spend in the China-Burma-India theater of operation. I never remember him talking much about the war except for one subject: Studebaker trucks. Studebaker manufactured most of the trucks used in the China-Burma-India campaigns and they were the workhorses used when the famous Burma Road was rebuilt to supply the Chinese nationalists in their fight against the Japanese occupation of their homeland. My Uncle Jim swore those were the best trucks ever made.

In the late 1940s after my uncle returned from the war to the farm, his father needed to buy a new farm truck. Of course, the truck had to be a Studebaker. When I visited on the farm, which was often, I would ride in that truck with my uncle everywhere he went. As I entered my teens and was learning to drive, Uncle Jim used that truck to teach me how to use a standard shift. I am not sure what became of that Studebaker farm truck, but I remember it well.

The truck I was standing next to was a replica of Uncle Jim's and his parents' farm truck. It had dual tandem back wheels, a flathead six cylinder engine, and in the front fenders it had what I had always called frog eyes (bulging headlight sockets) when I was young. Rust had eaten away most of the paint but I could still see flakes of the original colors; red on the body and black on the fenders; just like Uncle Jim's. All the comparisons indicated to me that the two trucks had been manufactured at about the same time—in the late 1940s. All of Studebaker's production capacity during the war was dedicated to making military trucks, so this truck had definitely been produced in that post-war period.

The door on the driver's side was swung back on its hinges, so I had a full view of the inside of the cab. There wasn't a whole lot left because of the fire. I noticed pieces of broken jars in the floor and assumed they must have come from mason jars that held the moonshine the occupants had drunk. Using my walking stick I probed the front seat springs to make sure no snakes were present. The springs had once been covered by fabric but only small remnants remained hanging from the frame.

It didn't look like humans had visited the truck over the years, because there were no telltale beer cans, soda cans, plastic soda bottles, and like garbage laying around. It must have been too far down the embankment for people to climb down to see it. On the other hand, bullets fired from apparently the top of the cliff had pretty well decimated the interior.

Most of the dashboard and glove box had fallen to the floor as well as had the sun visors. Again, using my walking stick I moved that junk around on what was left of the metal floorboards. While doing so, I spied what appeared to be a couple of small round black objects on the floor directly under where the glove box would have been in the dashboard. My curiosity took over and I pushed the objects with my stick. They were not affixed to anything and moved when I pushed them. After one last check for snakes in the cab of the truck, I reached in and picked up the two objects. They appeared to be some type of copper or brass coins that had been blackened and encrusted with grime over time. They were so blackened that I couldn't tell what denomination they were. I stuck them in my pocket and continued my inspection.

My mind kept wandering back to the broken glass from the mason jars. Something didn't seem quite right but I couldn't put my finger on it. I figured a break might relax my mind so I leaned up against a tree, unwrapped one of the orange/cranberry high-protein energy bars I had brought along, and stared through the door at the broken glass.

Before long the relaxing must have cleared my mind because I realized what was nagging at me. There were no jar lids anywhere to be found. Based on the amount of rounded broken glass, there must have been quite a few jars of moonshine in the cab of that truck when it went over the cliff. My reasoning told me that if two individuals had drunk that much potent moonshine prior to the wreck, they would have been totally comatose and unable to even drive up the mountain. On the other hand, if they hadn't drunk all that moonshine, the lids would have still been on some of the jars. If that were the case, when the jars broke the lids should be laying around with the other glass and wreckage. There were no lids!

As I climbed back up to my pickup, my thoughts turned to another question I had. Why were those guys driving up the mountain in the first place? Even today, except for one convenience store, there isn't a lot of entertainment on top of Keith Springs Mountain. I could only suppose there were fewer attractions there in the early 1950s. So again I asked myself, Why were they up there? If they were heading back to Texas, Rowe Gap Road would have been about the worst route they could have taken.

In the early 1950s the interstate highway system as we know it today didn't exist. It only came into being in the mid-1950s during President Eisenhower's administration and was patterned after the German autobahn system, which was designed to connect urban locations. Our interstate system, with even-numbered highways running east/west and odd numbered highways running north/south, was also designed to move troops quickly about the country, should war touch our shores.

Without interstate highways to travel on in 1951, if the truck was going back to Texas, there were better routes to take than going over Keith Springs Mountain and heading down into the maze of roads in northern Alabama. They could have taken U.S. Route 41 to Nashville and turned south, or a better alternative would have been to take U.S. Highway 64 from Winchester to Memphis, Tennessee and turn south from there.

When I got back up to the top, I stowed my gear in the pickup and headed home with more questions than I had answers. When I got home Gator was sulking because I hadn't taken him with me. Mary was upset because I had forgotten to call and tell her I was on my way home so she could start supper. Gator got over it quickly after a few pats on the head and a backrub. I had to take Mary out to supper before she would brighten up.

Before we went out to supper, I poured a can of Coke into a glass and dropped the two coins in it to soak. From my experience, Coke will clean about anything if given time, which has always caused me to wonder what it does to my stomach when I drink it.

•Chapter 18•

Mary and I treated ourselves to dinner "up on the mountain" in Monteagle, Tennessee at the High Point Restaurant. Anyone who has ever traveled on I-24 between Nashville and Chattanooga is familiar with where Monteagle is situated. It sits atop the Cumberland Plateau at exits 134 and 135 and is known for the steep uphill and downhill highway grades as you approach or depart the town. That stretch of interstate is one of the most dangerous in the United States, especially for truckers who have lost their brakes on the downhill portions of the road. Johnny Cash even wrote a song about the dangers of crossing over Monteagle Mountain. Technically there is no Monteagle Mountain; that is just the name of the town on top of that portion of the plateau. Though, when you drive that route, you are convinced you are crossing over a mountain.

Just like there are infamous stories about truckers who have been lost on that roadway, the stone building that houses the High Point Restaurant has infamous stories associated with it. Before the interstate highways were built, U.S. Route 41 passed through Monteagle. If a person in those days was traveling from Chicago to Miami, they would travel on Highway 41. One of the most infamous of those travelers who made Monteagle a stopover point was the gangster Al Capone. The High Point building was a residential home at the time and that is supposedly where Capone stayed. One story that persists to this day is that Al Capone slept upstairs in the house. Because he slept upstairs, he had the floors reinforced with additional lumber. So if unannounced visitors entered the first floor of the house while he was sleeping and fired bullets through the upstairs floor, he would be protected.

Mary and I choose the High Point Restaurant not for the stories surrounding the building, but because the meals are great. Both of us enjoyed High Point's lobster bisque. Then I partook of my favorite entrée, the High Point Oscar (steak topped with crabmeat) with asparagus, while Mary had their coconut shrimp.

When we returned home there were two messages on the answering machine. Brett had called to say he was back in town to help his mother with some financial matters, and Ted Carlson left a message to call him back in the morning to discuss some interesting information he had gotten from his friend at TVA headquarters.

I made a note to call them both in the morning.

CHAPTER 19

GATOR AND I WENT fishing the next morning. When we got home, we had a pleasant surprise; our daughter Mandy had the day off from the hospital and decided to join us for breakfast. That especially pleased Gator because he knew Mandy was likely to feed him people food under the table and Mary and I wouldn't.

Following breakfast, I called Ted.

"Good morning, Ted. I got your message last night and I thought I might catch you this morning before you got too busy."

"Busy is not the word for it. We've been swamped with applications for dock permits. I think it's related to all you *old baby boomers* retiring and buying vacation homes on the lake. Don't you all know that there is still some room left in Florida?" he laughed. "It would make my life a lot less hectic."

"Mr. Carlson," I replied, trying to sound serious and not laugh. "My tax dollars keep civil servants like you employed. If it wasn't for us *old geezers*, you wouldn't have a job."

"Touché," he replied. "I'll tell you what, my friend. Chuck told me something, but please don't say where you got the information. I don't believe it is meant for the general public."

"That's not a problem," I replied.

"Anyway, here is what Chuck said. The purchase of the property from Miller never took place, as you know, because he died. According to notes in the file, after his death no trustee's notice or letter of testamentary was ever filed or published in the paper. He was buried in a pauper's grave in Winchester because no one claimed his body. Without any survivor information, TVA couldn't identify his next of kin. They referred it to TVA's security department in hopes they might be able to locate a relative of Miller. According to our file notes, a deputy with the Franklin County Sheriff's Department who was interviewed said Miller might have had a brother or family in Brownsville, Texas."

"That deputy was probably Red Nelson," I interjected.

"I'm not sure who the deputy was because I haven't seen the file myself; but Chuck told me the security department's effort to locate a relative was unsuccessful. The bottom line is, TVA found no one to close the deal with."

"So who got the money for the farm," I asked.

"No one," Ted replied. "The money is still gathering dust, being held in escrow, waiting for someone to claim it. Chuck said there were a couple other similar cases to this one but they were settled years ago. Maybe you could grow a beard, learn to speak German, and claim the money," he added teasingly.

"That's a good plan but Gator can't understand German," I added. "He would give me away."

CHAPTER 20

AFTER I THANKED TED for his help, I called Brett. His mom, Sally, answered.

"Sally, how are you doing? I understand your vagabond son came in yesterday."

"He sure did and it's great to have him, even if it's just for a few days. Vicki left day before yesterday and I miss her already."

"Would you and Brett be interested in joining Mary, Mandy, and me for lunch?" I asked. "I was thinking about getting a po' boy over at the Blue Gill Grill at Holiday Marina."

"I'm going to have to pawn Brett off on you for that," she replied. "I promised June Sanders I would go with her to Sir's in Fayetteville to shop for fabric she needs for some curtains she is making. But I appreciate the invitation. Do you want me to put Brett on the line?"

"Thanks, Sally. We will see you later," I said and then waited for Brett.

I heard a discussion in the background and then Brett picked up the phone.

"Uncle Rick, you've saved my day. I love my mom, but a po' boy and a cold beer sound much better than shopping with two ladies for material. That's what she was about to rope me into."

"I'm glad I could save the day. How about we pick you up around twelve o'clock?" I asked.

"That will work fine. Gives me time for my daily run and a shower. See you then," he replied and hung up.

I walked out on the porch to tell Mary about the lunch plan and make sure Mandy could join us.

Mandy thought for a moment, glanced at her mom, and then suggested, "It is a gorgeous day. Why don't you and mom ride your Harley over? I can pick up Brett and we can join you."

I had just started explaining it would not make sense to take two vehicles when I got the evil eye from Mary. I am not sure how a wife's evil eye is interrupted in other households, but in ours it means *please shut you mouth my dear; we will talk about it later!*

"Mandy, that sounds like a great plan," I meekly said, and then moved to the den to await further instructions from my better half.

As I walked into the den a thought struck me that I forgot to check the coins. I headed to the garage, where I had left them.

I poured the Coke out and looked into the bottom of the glass. The Coke had done its job. The coins weren't in mint condition but they appeared to be a lot cleaner than when they entered the glass. I dumped them onto a rag and wiped them off before I picked one of them up. I was hoping they might be old buffalo nickels or mercury dimes. What I found surprised me.

On the back of the coin I picked up off the rag, I found the denomination—fifty centimos—and a wreath on the border. I turned it over and on the front of the coin I saw a lion, the year 1948, the words *paz y justicia*, which in Spanish mean "peace and justice." And most surprisingly, I found the words *republlica del paraquay*. The other coin was similar in all aspects except for the year—1947.

Evidently, the truck and possibly its occupants had been in Paraguay at one time or another. That was really an unexpected development. Because the license tags were stolen in Brownsville, Texas, I was making the mistake of assuming the truck must have come from Mexico. Now it appeared that the truck could have crossed through Mexico, but its origination point may have been elsewhere.

By then the morning was slipping away and I needed to discuss the evil eye with my wife before we left for lunch.

•CHAPTER 21•

When I walked back into the house Mandy was in our bedroom going through Mary's closet, so I had the opportunity to pull Mary aside and talk to her.

"Dearest, what was the evil eye for when I was in here earlier? I don't think I said anything out of line."

"Rick, you are a good husband and father. But there are some things men just can't understand. Can't you see why your sweet daughter wants us to drive separately?" she asked.

"Hon, I figured she wanted you and me to have some time alone on this beautiful day. Not a bad idea I might add," I said as I gave Mary a hug.

She responded with a smile and said, "You got it half right. The alone part was correct; you got the couple she wants to be alone wrong."

"I still do not understand," I said with a puzzled look.

"How can my husband be so smart in most subjects but sometimes so dense where his daughters are concerned? Think about it. Brett is handsome and single. Mandy is beautiful and single."

"Oh! You're right! I guess fathers are the last to understand. Go get ready for lunch and I'll get the bike out of the garage."

My bike was a mid-life gift to myself. It's the Harley Davidson Electra Glide touring model. It is great for Mary and me when we want to take a few hours off and tour the back roads of Tennessee. We appreciate it the most in the fall, when nature has painted the trees in an autumn palette of glorious colors. Much of the time we pack a picnic lunch in the fiberglass saddle bags, put a small cooler in the tour pack on the back, put a Bonnie Raitt CD in the CD Player, and head out for a day of relaxation.

By the time Mary was ready—decked out in what she calls her "traveling leather" (chaps, jacket, and all)—Mandy had already left to pick up Brett. I cranked up the bike and we headed over to join them at the Blue Gill Grill.

The Blue Gill Grill is actually a floating restaurant at the Holiday Marina. The menu is varied enough to accommodate all tastes and the atmosphere on the outside deck is casual and relaxed. After we had ordered our sandwiches, with a cold beer for the guys and wine coolers for the girls, I asked Brett if he could join me back at the house for an hour or so after lunch.

"Mom won't get home from shopping until about six o'clock, so I am free," Brett replied as Mandy smiled in the background. "Does this have to do with the concerns you mentioned at our house after the break-in?"

"You know me. Having been involved in investigations for so many years causes me to read more into things than perhaps I should. I've looked into some things since I talked to you after your father's death and I have more questions now then I had then. I would like to outline what I have found and get your opinion."

Mary reminded me, "We are going to the Chambers' house for dinner tonight but we don't have to be there until seven o'clock. Hopefully that won't interfere with your plans."

"Brett and I will be done before then. It wouldn't take us long. We don't have anything planned for tomorrow night, do we?" I asked Mary.

"Nothing I am aware of. Are you going to be doing something?" she inquired as she took a sip of her wine cooler.

"Yep, I'm going back to Verne's Pool to find out more about those lights, or whatever they are. If they're down there tomorrow night, I have a plan that might flush out whoever or whatever is down there. If you want to go fishing you have to bait the hook. I plan on baiting the hook," I responded.

"Dad! You're retired! You do not need to be running around on the lake in the middle of the night looking for something you don't know anything about," Mandy said in an exasperated tone of voice. "Mom, please talk to him."

"It wouldn't do any good. When he has made up his mind about something, nothing changes his mind." Mary sounded as exasperated as my daughter.

"Brett, how are things in Washington?" I interjected in a feeble attempt to change the subject.

After an excellent lunch, the four of us arrived back at the house at about the same time.

Before Brett and I retired to the den, Mandy had a request. "Mom and Dad, Brett is only going to be in town for a few days and we want to take the two of you and his mom to Riverbend for dinner. With our schedules, it looks like tomorrow night is the only night we can do it. Is that okay?"

Mary piped up before I could say anything. "Tomorrow night will be fine. We haven't been out with Sally since…uh, in a while. It will be fun. Rick, you will just have to delay your outing on the lake one night."

I knew at that point there was no arguing, so I grabbed Brett and we headed into the den.

•Chapter 22•

When Brett and I were seated comfortably on the couch, I pulled the coffee table up close and opened my notebook. Before I could say anything, Brett opened our discussion.

"Uncle Rick, tell me what you plan to do on the lake two nights from now."

"Some things are better left unsaid," I replied. "Trust me, I have a plan."

"I'll still be in town. Will you let me join you?" Brett asked.

"Thanks, but your mother would shoot me for dragging you away. If I need your help later, I'll let you know. For right now, I need to handle it myself."

I then turned the subject back to what I had asked Brett to stop by to discuss: the information I had uncovered since his father's death.

"Brett, for the basis of our discussion, I have no doubt that your dad observed something or someone at Verne's Pool. I questioned it—thought maybe he had seen reflections on the water or something like that. But I saw the lights or glow myself and it definitely comes from underwater.

Based on my findings, I typed up these notes to help me make some rhyme or reason out of all this. Let's look at them so I can get your thoughts," I added as I showed him my notes.

- *Johnny drowns without a life vest and his GPS and cell phone are missing.*

"This note has to do with what we discussed after the funeral," I explained. "Like I alluded to then, I am not convinced that your father died accidentally. He always wore his life vest. Plus, he would have no reason to be moving around in the boat with his GPS in his hand if he was anchoring the boat. But that is what Captain King seems to believe happened."

Brett commented on that point. "I know one thing. My father was a fighter. If foul play was involved in his death, there should have been some sign of a struggle. He wouldn't have gone down without a fight."

"Brett, I couldn't agree with you more. Then again, I saw no signs of a struggle and that may be partially the reason Captain King didn't request an autopsy. Although there was no apparent sign of a struggle, I still do not subscribe to the accidental drowning theory."

My next notes had to do with the research I did at the library and my interviews with Tony G. and Red Nelson. I first reviewed with Brett those notes pertaining to Ike Marshall and the Marshall farm.

- *My research at the library showed the GPS location Johnny called Verne's Pool corresponded to the underwater location of the old Marshall farm.*

- *Miller, as a POW, had worked for Ike Marshall during the war.*

- *Miller returned to work for Ike in the post-war years.*

- *Ike was killed in an accident on the night of January 6, 1951. It was supposed to be alcohol related but nothing indicated Ike had a drinking problem.*

- *Miller purchased the farm with cash, although he only was paid a farmhand's salary.*

"There is no doubt in my mind that the old Marshall farm is the underwater location of your dad's Verne's Pool. Helmut Miller was a German POW at Camp Forrest during World War II. He worked for Ike Marshall during the day on some type of work release program," I explained. "After the war, Miller went back to Germany, then returned and again worked for Ike. Ike Marshall died in an alcohol related accident but apparently didn't have a drinking problem. Miller benefited by buying the farm from Ike's granddaughter. I found it interesting that he paid cash for the farm but had no apparent means of income other than a farmhand's wage."

"Uncle Rick," Brett asked, "After World War II, wasn't the German currency that anyone would have accumulated before the war practically worthless?"

"From everything I've read that is correct. The whole country had to be rebuilt, including the economy," I answered.

Brett continued that train of thought. "Then Miller would have had no money to bring back with him when he returned here after the war. If he was prosperous enough to have the amount of money required to buy the farm, why would he work as a farmhand? All that leads me to the same question you have, Uncle Rick: Where did Miller's money come from?"

The look of puzzlement on Brett's face grew as I overviewed the next items in my notes.

- *There was a truck delivery to Miller from Texas, after which the drivers died on Keith Springs Mountain. There were no witnesses, no apparent reason for them to be in that vicinity, and the accident was amazingly similar to the way Ike Marshall died.*

- *The truck had come through Texas supposedly with furniture. I originally thought it came from Mexico. Then again, it may have come through Mexico from South America, based on the finding of the coins from Paraguay.*

"Brett, that truck is still there at the base of a cliff up on Keith Springs Mountain. I climbed down to it and there is not much left of it. Following my discussions with Deputy Nelson, I thought the truck had come up from Mexico through Texas. However, that was before I found two coins in the truck from Paraguay. Perhaps that truck came up from South America rather than Mexico."

I added a couple of other concerns. "Tony Gladson's nephew built a cistern for Miller. While doing so, he had occasion to be in Miller's house and saw Miller's furniture. The nephew's opinion was the furniture wasn't worth moving across town, much less all the way from Texas. If furniture wasn't delivered, what was?

"Deputy Nelson also told me that Miller had a brother visiting at the time of the truck wreck and delivery of the furniture," I continued. "The brother was not helpful to the sheriff or Deputy Nelson. If the brother had helped arrange moving the furniture, why wouldn't he have spoken up and cleared up the questions the sheriff had?"

I also shared the rest of my truck wreck concerns with Brett, like why the truck was on the mountain in the first place, where were the lids for the jars, etc.

Before I could go further Brett asked another question. "Uncle Rick, you'll have to excuse my ignorance, but remember I was raised in cities. You mentioned that Tony Gladson's nephew built a cistern on the farm. What exactly is a cistern?"

"Brett, I forgot you were a city boy," I said, laughing. "Cisterns are normally built below ground level with poured concrete or concrete blocks. They are made watertight and are designed to catch rainwater from downspouts on houses or whatever. The water they hold is then used as the main source of water for a home or to supplement another water source, such as a well, during dry seasons."

I added, "Don't think that is a stupid question. You have always lived where city water lines were available, so you never saw a cistern. My uncle had one on their farm and they sometimes had to use the water stored in it during the summer months."

After explaining what a cistern was, I started reviewing my final notes. From the anxious look on his face, I could tell that Brett was intrigued with what we had discussed up to that point.

"My remaining questions are reflected in these final five points I have written," I told Brett. "They pretty well sum things up."

- *Miller died of snakebite before TVA bought the land and no next of kin were found or notified.*

- *Johnny saw lights at Verne's Pool.*

- *Johnny's house was broken into after the boating "accident" but only the computer was taken, although other valuables were there.*

- *The only links between the computer and GPS were the fish beds and Verne's Pool locations.*

- *I visited Verne's Pool and verified what Johnny had observed.*

After reviewing the remaining five notes, I said to Brett, "The link to everything seems to be the lights your dad saw at Verne's Pool. Someone or something is down there generating light. If they are human, which I happen to believe they are because I don't believe in science fiction, then what are they doing down there?" I concluded by saying, "I have either let my imagination run away with itself or something bad wrong is happening."

Brett was quiet for quite a while and I could tell he was pondering everything we had discussed. Then he spoke.

"Uncle Rick, please let me have a blank piece of paper. I have some thoughts going through my head and I want to capture them on paper as we talk."

I handed Brett a page from my notebook and he began making some notes.

"The first thing we know for sure is there is something or someone moving around at Verne's Pool. Based on your and dad's observations, we also know it seems to confine itself to the area that was the old Marshall farm," Brett said as he wrote. "In addition, we know that there were a series of accidents which now appear suspicious," he added.

"Make a note of this," I instructed. "What is the common thread or threads between these events?"

Brett thought for a moment and then asked, "Would you agree that the farm and Miller are two common threads?"

I acknowledged my agreement with Brett's observation and added a question of my own. "It goes back to the question I have had all along: What would be so important about Miller or the farm that would cause someone to take your dad's life?"

"Uncle Rick, I don't know the answer to that. For a minute, let's confine ourselves to what my dad knew. From what you have outlined, I believe all he knew was the location of Verne's Pool and that there were some sort of lights down there. If they killed my dad, they must have not wanted anyone to know they were down there. Is it possible they are hunting for something left behind by Miller?" Brett speculated.

"I would say that is a good possibility," I added, while observing that Brett and I had begun to refer to the source of the Verne's Pool lights as being generated by someone, not something.

Brett was again deep in thought and I didn't interrupt him until he spoke again.

"You said a few minutes ago, 'If furniture wasn't delivered, what was?' If they are hunting for something, I don't believe it would be a stretch to surmise that what they are hunting for was delivered in the truck from south of the border. Let's think about it. The witnesses (drivers of the truck) died immediately after the delivery. Miller had someone there at the house that he identified as his brother, who could help him stage the wreck and get him back home."

"We could carry your thought a step further," I added. "Miller died unexpectedly and TVA flooded the valley before any next of kin could be notified. If something was hidden on the farm, no one other than Miller may have known it needed to be removed, until it was too late."

"I would say that is a solid theory," Brett said in agreement. He also reflected. "Haven't there always been stories circulated after World War II about German officials, German treasures, Artwork, bio-technology secrets, secret weapon technology, etcetera, disappearing into South America?"

I agreed with my godson's observation and told him, "That is a direction I need to pursue. I'll do some research on the Internet and see what I can find. In the meantime, I need to get ready for dinner with the Chambers. What time will we see you tomorrow?"

"Will it be okay if Mom and I pick you and Aunt Mary up around four o'clock? Then we can pick Mandy up in Tullahoma on our way to Shelbyville."

"That should work just fine. Also, right now let's not discuss with your mom our concerns regarding your dad's death," I said as I walked with him into the living room and left him with Mandy.

I then hurried into the bedroom to change clothes for dinner and hopefully to find some time to start my Internet research before it was time to leave.

·CHAPTER 23·

THE FOLLOWING DAY I awoke early and spent most of the day on the Internet. I started my research by reviewing post-war Nuremberg trial records to determine which German officials might have escaped from Germany. What I found astounded me. The second highest official in the Third Reich, second only to Adolph Hitler, was never officially accounted for after the war.

Martin Bormann was chief of staff and top aide to the Führer until Hitler's death. According to documentation, he was present on April 30, 1945 in the Berlin Führerbunker when Hitler committed suicide after directing that his body be cremated with gasoline by his own people. Following Hitler's death, Bormann was elevated to head of the National Socialist German Workers Party (NSDAP or Nazi Party). He then disappeared and there have been controversies surrounding his disappearance that exist to this day. One school of thought is that he escaped to South America with the purpose of continuing the struggle for world dominance by the Third Reich. I found a tremendous amount of information and speculation that supports that theory.

Bormann was alleged to have been sighted in several South American countries in the post World War II years. Argentina, Peru, Venezuela, and Paraguay were four of the countries that I found were most associated with Bormann sightings. I also noticed that most of the Bormann encounters occurred in the late 1940s and 1950s. I found no documented sightings that took place in the 1960s. Based on Bormann's age at the time of his disappearance and lack of 1960 sightings, my assumption was that Bormann must have died sometime in the late 1950s.

Associated with narratives of Bormann's disappearing to South America, I found stories of how the continued struggle for world domination would be financed. According to what I read, prior to the end of the war, most German officials saw the writing on the wall and could foresee Germany's ultimate defeat. With that thought in mind, they undertook the task of moving what German treasures they could out of the country. Included in those treasures were gold and silver bullion, coins, jewels, and works of art. According to many individuals involved in the transfer of the wealth, it was designated to go to South America and be placed under the control of Martin Bormann for use in a long-term clandestine effort to topple their arch enemy, the government of the United States.

In April 1945, the United States Third Army found a great amount of gold bullion and currency hidden in a salt mine near Merkers, Germany. An inventory of that find does not indicate that any art works or jewels were found. I found further information that the gold bullion found in the salt mine represented only a small portion of total German gold treasure.

If I was astounded by the information I initially found, I was dumfounded by what I found next. I could not wait to share my findings with Brett.

•CHAPTER 24•

PROMPTLY AT FOUR O'CLOCK that afternoon, Brett and his mom, Sally, picked us up at our house for dinner at the Riverbend Country Club in Shelbyville, Tennessee. On the way north on Highway 41A, we stopped in Tullahoma to pick up Mandy at her house. While Brett went to the door, Mary and Sally couldn't resist commenting on what a cute couple they made. I believe their secret hopes were for a romance to develop that would eventually produce a marriage and beautiful grandchildren they could share. Of course, Sally and Mary's wishful thinking would not come to fruition without Brett and Mandy's cooperation. Knowing how independent each was, I wasn't expecting wedding bells to ring anytime in the near future. Still, what does a father know?

After we picked up Mandy, we continued another twenty miles or so up the road to Shelbyville.

Shelbyville, Tennessee is the county seat for Bedford County, Tennessee and is the Tennessee Walking Horse Capital of the World. The Tennessee Walking Horse National Celebration is held there every year for eleven days in the summer and ends on the Saturday night before Labor Day. Locally, it is known simply as "the celebration" and attracts around a quarter-million visitors each year from around the world. The celebration complex includes a 30,000-seat outdoor stadium, a warm-up arena, and a 4,400-seat indoor arena. With 63 barns with 1,650 stalls, it can accommodate most of the horses competing in the shows.

The bloodlines for the Tennessee Walking Horse extends back over 100 years to 1885, and over the years this magnificent breed of horse has won the hearts of horse lovers everywhere. It was the first horse in the United States to be named after a state. During the shows, the horses and riders demonstrate three gaits to the pleasure of the crowd—the flat-foot walk, running walk, and canter.

The canter is sometimes referred to as the "rocking chair gait" and is the high-stepping trademark gait of the Tennessee Walking Horse. When performed by these beautiful horses, you can almost always be assured the crowd will come to their feet, clapping together in appreciation of the performance.

After we entered Shelbyville, we doubled-back on Highway 130 to reach the Riverbend Country Club. By this time I was hungry and anxious to enjoy the finely prepared meals that can always be found at the club (which is how most locals refer to Riverbend Country Club).

The club was established 1959 and the course was designed by the famous golf course architect George Cobb, who designed over 350 golf courses during his career. It was once a 300-acre farm overlooking a bend on the scenic Duck River—hence the name Riverbend.

Like in many smaller towns in southern states, the country club is the center for many of the social events that take place. Riverbend is no exception. Besides golfing, the club is available for wedding receptions, fraternal and social club meetings, fundraisers, and just about any other event that might take place in the town.

After Brett parked and we entered the dining room, Mary and Sally spied a friend of theirs from the garden club. We stopped at her table to say hello. Pam Beasley and her husband Rick grew up in the Shelbyville area, left and made their mark in the business world, and had returned to Shelbyville a few years ago to enjoy their early retirement. Pam and their beautiful daughter Katie have the distinction of representing two generations of Walking Horse celebration queens. Pam was queen of the celebration in 1971 and Katie was queen in 2000. Obviously, husband and father Rick Beasley is very proud of his southern ladies.

We were enjoying our meal and the friendly atmosphere of Riverbend, but I remained on the lookout for an opportunity to speak to Brett alone. That opportunity came when the girls left the table at the same time to go over and speak to a friend of Sally's at another table.

"Brett, I found some amazing information today when I was doing research on the Internet. In fact, you will not believe what I found. There is a possibility that Miller wasn't who everyone thought he was. Are you free tomorrow afternoon to come by the house so we can go over it?"

Brett looked away and I thought I detected a look of avoidance in his eyes. I felt perhaps my theories may have become too farfetched for him to accept.

When he turned back toward me, he replied to my question, "I'm not really free tomorrow afternoon. How about sometime in the morning?" Again, he dropped his eyes and it seemed to me his mind was wandering elsewhere.

"Sure, tomorrow morning will be fine. Anytime after eight o'clock will be all right by me," I quickly said, just as the girls were returning to the table.

On the drive home from the club, we all talked about normal things such as how pleasant the weather was for that time of year. However, I sensed that Brett was quieter than I normally knew him to be. After he and Sally dropped Mary and I off at the house, I was still wondering what was on his mind.

•CHAPTER 25•

I WAS UP EARLY the next day and planned for a busy time. I was meeting with Brett that morning and I had to assemble my gear for my return to Verne's Pool that night. When Brett arrived around nine o'clock I was excited to share with him the information I had discovered from my research. Again, I had made notes and shared a copy of my first seven bulleted items with Brett.

- *Martin Bormann was second in command to Hitler and headed the Nazi Party after Hitler's death.*

- *Bormann disappeared after the war.*

- *Bormann was rumored to have gone to South America to continue the quest for Nazi world domination and the overthrow of the United States government.*

- *Sightings of Bormann included the countries of Argentina, Peru, Venezuela, and Paraguay.*

- *Bormann's efforts were to be financed by German treasures.*

- *Alleged German treasures such as art works and gold and silver bullion in bars and ingots, coins, jewels, etc. were never fully accounted for in the post-war period.*

- *Sightings and rumors of Bormann in South America stopped in the late 1950s.*

After Brett had time to digest the information contained in my Bormann notes, we discussed them.

"If any of this information is true, it appears to me that a large amount of funds left Germany before or after the end of the war and went with Bormann to South America," I said.

Brett added, "It would appear that way. And I think it is significant that one of Bormann's goals was the overthrow of the United States." He continued by saying, "Let me be the devil's advocate for a minute and ask some critical questions. How does the possibility of Bormann's existence in South America after World War II and German treasures relate to Tims Ford Lake, the old Marshall farm, or for that matter, Miller?"

"The answer to those questions may involve what else I discovered. Look at these notes," I stated.

- *Bormann had an aide-de-camp until early 1942. From 1942 until after the end of the war, the aide was not sighted with Bormann or heard from.*

- *Information indicated the aide was captured by American forces but his name did not appear on any POW rosters.*

- *After the war, for a short period of time the aide reappeared with Bormann in South America.*

- *He then again disappeared in the late 1940s and there is no record of his existence from that point forward.*

"I am not trying to be critical," Brett said with a tone of apology in his voice. "But again, I don't really see a connection here."

"I didn't either until I found the name of the aide-de-camp," I explained. "His name was Helmut Müller. It seemed coincidental that he and Miller both had the same first name." I went on to explain, "You know I don't believe much in coincidences, so on a hunch, I ran their last names through a German/English translation dictionary on the Internet. Müller is a common surname in Germany. In German its meaning is *miller*, as in someone who mills grain."

Brett got up from the couch and walked around the room for a couple of minutes and I didn't disturb his thoughts. When he came back to the couch, he sat down but remained silent for a while longer.

Pretty soon he spoke up. "The ramifications of this could be tremendous. Correct me if I am wrong, but what I am seeing is that Miller and Müller may have been one in the same. That is mind-boggling."

I agreed. "I think that is a good possibility. If true, many of the pieces of the puzzle would fit together. Here is a scenario to think about," I said as I started writing bullet points on a sheet of paper.

- *Müller is captured and changes his name to Miller to hide his true identity from American forces.*

- *Müller (now Miller) is sent to Camp Forrest as a POW and works on the farm for Ike Marshall.*

- *Müller joins up with Bormann after the war.*

- *Bormann wants a base of operations in the United States.*

- *Because of his high profile, it is too dangerous for Bormann to run the U.S. operation himself. So he puts Müller in charge.*

At that point Brett jumped in and added his own bullet point to the paper.

- *Müller kills Ike and buys the farm.*

"That would explain how Müller/Miller got the cash to buy the farm," I interjected as we continued listing bullet items on our sheet.

- *German treasure is transported here from South America to fund the Nazi takeover effort in the United States.*

- *Truck drivers are killed to eliminate witnesses.*

"Hang on a minute," Brett said. "An idea just crossed my mind. Bormann seemed to have had a great deal of resources available to him in order for him to move around like he did. Is it feasible that Bormann entered the United States to oversee whatever might have been shipped up from South America?"

My mind was tracking with the scenario and I said, "If Bormann came here, that could account for who Müller/Miller's visiting brother was. It could have been Bormann."

"Didn't Müller/Miller die about the same time Bormann was no longer heard from?" Brett asked.

"I see where you are going with that. If Müller/Miller died before he was able to talk to Bormann, or if Bormann was already dead, no one would have known that the farm was going to be submerged under over 100 feet of water."

"In that case, whatever was down there is still down there and it seems someone is hunting for it!" Brett excitedly exclaimed.

"It also appears they haven't found it yet; otherwise they would be gone," he added.

"To test our theory, we need to know who the hunters are and what they are hunting for. Most importantly, we need to know if they were involved in any way with your father's death. I plan to start the process of gathering that information tonight," I said.

"Uncle Rick, I'll be honest with you. You won't let me help you tonight and I am afraid you might be John Wayneing things. I know you don't want something to happen to me," he said, and then added. "What if something happens to you? How would I explain that to Aunt Mary and Mandy?"

"Brett, John Wayne, in his life, played in movies. In my life, I have played for real! Trust me, I don't plan on doing anything stupid. Now, let's see if your Aunt Mary can rustle us up some lunch before you leave—if you have time?"

Brett stood up from the couch, put his arm around my shoulders, and said, "I may not be going with you tonight, but I'll be with you."

I assumed he meant *in spirit only*.

•CHAPTER 26•

THAT NIGHT AROUND NINE o'clock I loaded a few items in my boat and prepared to head out to Verne's Pool. The sky was cloudy and overcast but no rain was forecast. Gator was at the dock and eager to join me.

"I'm sorry, buddy, but you have to stay home on this trip. I'll take you next time."

Mary wasn't too happy about me going out alone. Nonetheless, she still came down to the dock to give me a kiss and hug and a reminder to be careful. After assuring her I would be safe, I headed downriver.

It was about 9:30 when I reached Verne's Pool and I planned to use the same procedures to search for the underwater lights that I had the last time I was there. My plan was to peer down into the water every fifteen minutes or so searching for lights. I didn't have long to wait. On my first search, I saw lights moving deep below the surface.

Upon spotting the lights, I immediately started to implement my plan to get the attention of whomever or whatever was down there. When I had visited the Fireworks Superstore a few days previously, my intent was to purchase some M-80 cherry bombs. Unfortunately, things had changed since I was a teenager and I found they didn't manufacture powerful M-80 cherry bombs anymore. I had to take what the clerk described as the next best thing—M-150 maximum-load firecrackers. The M-150 is about the size of my little finger. Small as they are, they still pack a wallop.

At the house I had also taken a five-foot piece of PVC pipe I had leftover from a project and capped one end of it. By submerging the capped end down into the water and dropping a lit M-150 into it, when the firecracker exploded, the concussion would create a shock wave that would trigger a disturbance in the water. My desire was that the disturbance would cause whatever was down in the water to investigate where the explosions were coming from. In that manner, I might be able to bring the source of the light to me.

I put my plan into operation by exploding ten M-150s in the PVC pipe, one at a time. I then went to the front of the boat and peered down into the water to see if anything had changed. The only change I noted was what I could no longer observe. The lights had gone out.

With no more lights below the surface, I figured it was time to start a waiting game. Hopefully, they would come to me. I took a seat in the captain's chair on my boat and waited.

While waiting, I observed everything that was happening on top of the water, which wasn't much. A pontoon boat came into the vicinity. It looked similar to the one I had seen trolling the last time I was at Verne's Pool. I was hoping the pontoon boat wouldn't scare away the light source like it had apparently done the last time I was there. After the pontoon boat made a pass over Verne's Pool, it rounded a bend in the lake and I lost track of it.

After about a half hour of no activity I was attempting to formulate another plan that might be more successful in bringing the lights to the surface. About then, my thoughts were interrupted by a fishing boat sputtering toward me with two fishermen in it. It was moving very slowly and was experiencing obvious engine problems.

When that boat was about fifty feet away from mine, the driver hailed me.

"Hey friend, we seem to be having a problem. Is there a possibility you might be able to tow us over to Tims Ford Marina."

There is an unwritten rule on the lake that if one is able to, one will attempt to assist a boat in distress. Therefore, I didn't give a second thought about trying to help.

"I can do that," I shouted. "Bring your boat alongside and we will lash them together. I prefer to tow your boat alongside me, rather than behind me with a long rope. It makes my boat easier to control."

"I'm Frank Snelling. Glad to meet you. What's your name?" the driver asked.

"I'm Rick Cheatham. Have you guys been out long tonight?" I asked as they pulled alongside.

"Not too long. We were out a couple hours at the most before this motor started acting up on us. Where do you live, Rick?"

"Right up Rock Creek after you cross the no wake zone by Tyler's Market," I replied, while observing that his passenger hadn't said a word.

When they pulled alongside, I also observed something in their boat that caused me to think twice about what they were up to. There was a University of Tennessee life vest on the floor in their boat. It appeared identical to the life vest that Johnny always wore.

My mind was racing. The first thing I needed to know was if these guys were legitimate or had used a ploy to get near my boat. I figured if they were UT fans, a UT question might be appropriate.

"I can tell by that life vest at least one of you is a UT fan. Do you think Fulmer will keep Mickey Andrews around for another year as his defensive coordinator?" I nonchalantly asked.

The driver again was the only one to respond. "I'm your UT fan. I think Fulmer will likely keep Andrews around."

Wrong answer! I had thrown out a loaded question as a test of their UT football knowledge and the driver had failed the test.

Football fans in the South take their football seriously. Any University of Tennessee fan would know that Mickey Andrews was not the defensive coordinator for UT. It was John Chavis who worked for UT Head Football Coach Phillip Fulmer. Mickey Andrews was defensive coordinator for Bobby Bowden at Florida State University in Tallahassee, Florida.

Perhaps they were involved in Johnny's drowning; perhaps they weren't. In either case, I had to know. Hopefully a ploy of my own would give me my answer.

I knew that Johnny had normally kept his cell phone in the pocket of his life vest when he was out in his boat. If that was Johnny's life vest in their boat, Johnny's cell phone might still be there.

I moved toward the center of my boat, and as I did, I told them, "Hang on a second. My cell phone is vibrating. I've got a call."

My phone wasn't really vibrating and I didn't have an incoming call. However, I used to call Johnny several times a week and had his number on my speed dial list.

I removed my cell phone from my jacket and pressed Johnny's speed dial number. A moment later, the "Rocky Top" (UT fight song) ringing tone I was so familiar with from my days with Johnny began to emit from, I was now certain, Johnny's cell phone in Johnny's life vest.

The ringing of Johnny's cell phone caught the two men in the other boat by surprise, but they were quick to recover. If I previously had any questions regarding their intent, those questions were erased when the passenger in the boat reached under his jacket and pulled out an automatic pistol and swung around in an attempt to aim it at me.

My reaction was to move to my left, hoping to put the driver of the boat between me and the passenger. For a couple of moments the passenger didn't have line of sight to me and couldn't fire without striking his partner first. Those couple of moments allowed me time to draw my Smith and Wesson Model 645 .45 caliber automatic and dive back to my right. As I did so, I heard the discharge of the passenger's weapon and heard it impact in the seat directly behind me. I also felt a burning sensation on the left side of my forehead and realized the bullet had grazed me in passing.

In a battle of any type, I've always learned that if the odds are against you; go on the offensive whenever possible. That is what I did. I crawled forward a few feet to change my position, then leaped up and dived into their boat. With all three of us now in the same boat, confusion reigned. I backhanded the driver with my pistol while at the same time bringing my knee up into the groin of the passenger. When the passenger bent over from the blow to his groin I was able to grab the pistol in his right hand and bend his hand backward until I felt a snap and heard a howl of pain. I tossed his pistol overboard, shoved him to the deck, and turned my attention back to the driver.

By then blood had obscured my vision in my left eye. Yet I was still able to see enough out of my right eye as I turned toward the driver to see his arm swing around, holding a strange looking square barreled pistol. Immediately it registered in my mind that what he was holding and attempting aim in my direction was a Taser gun.

Instinct told me I didn't have enough time to swing my automatic around and get a clear shot at him before he fired the Taser. Therefore, I attempted to dive back into my boat and evade his shot. If I was successful in avoiding the Taser shot, I knew I would have the advantage, because reloading a Taser gun in the middle of an encounter is not an option.

Unfortunately, I was not fast enough and I felt the Taser probes strike me in the back. As I was experiencing the immobilizing effects of the Taser and was about to black out, I was also conscious of hearing a loud bang and of seeing an extremely blight light that seemingly surrounded the two boats. Then darkness overcame me.

•Chapter 27•

I was drifting through clouds; some were bright and some were dark. Then I heard voices. At first the voices were far off in the distance. Then the voices were drawing nearer. My eyes fluttered open and I heard one of the voices say, "Get ready, Bear. He's coming around and may want to fight."

I tried to focus my eyes, but all I could see was a huge dark mass repeating some words I couldn't decipher. Again, I heard the other voice and this time I could understand more of what he said.

"Mr. Cheatham, you're okay. Bear and I've got things under control. Just relax now." Then I drifted off again.

At some point I again emerged into consciousness and realized my arms were pinned to my side. I attempted to fight off what was pinning me down but could gain no leverage.

Then I heard the dark mass that was holding me down say, "You don't know us but we are friends. Brett will be back real soon to explain everything. While we are waiting, we want you to rest easy. No one is going to hurt you anymore as long as Doc and I are here." He continued. "I am going to ease up on your arms now so we can get you in a more comfortable position. Please don't fight me."

By then I was able to see more clearly and focus on my surroundings. I was on the deck of my boat with a cushion propped up behind my head. A dark African American man was on my right side. He was a big man and his size reminded me of the character Hagrid in the Harry Potter movies. This must be Bear, I thought, because he fit the name so well.

The person on my left was slender and did not have the muscular bulk that Bear did. He was on his knees next to an open medic's bag and had been attending to the wound on my forehead. He had to be Doc.

By now I was awake enough to realize that these two individuals were only concerned about my welfare. I didn't know where they had come from or how they had gotten there, but I was happy they were there.

I sat up and asked a couple of obvious questions. "How long have I been out and how did the two of you get here?"

Bear spoke up in a gentle voice. "You've been out for about fifteen minutes. It's best that Brett answers your other question."

As he was speaking, I heard a boat approaching. I couldn't see it because my head was below the railing. From the sound of the motor, I assumed it was a smaller boat.

"Grab the line and tie us off. Has my Uncle Rick come to yet?" my godson Brett shouted.

"I can answer that," I yelled. "I'm awake but totally confused. Where did you and these guys come from?"

"Uncle Rick," Brett said as he stepped over the rail of the boat. "Meet some members of my team. You've met Bear and Doc. These two fine gentlemen behind me in our Zodiac are Tonto and Charlie."

Tonto and Charlie tied up their six-man military style Zodiac to the back of my boat and joined us.

"Brett, you are avoiding my question. Where did you all come from? Not that I'm sad you're here; I'm happy the cavalry arrived. I just don't understand how you got here."

"Remember lunch two days ago," Brett said. You were going to come here last night but I wasn't invited. I was concerned but couldn't get my guys here from DC with the Zodiac until today. Mandy helped me out there."

It dawned on me what he and my daughter had done. "On the drive back from the Blue Gill Grill, you and Mandy must have improvised by inviting us to dinner last night at the club. That way, you could buy another day to get your guys here. Pretty cute!"

"How did you know what was going to happen out here?" I asked him.

"I didn't. But I was fearful something like this was going to happen, and I wanted to be here to watch your back. That is why I couldn't meet with you this afternoon. We had to set up our observation post over there on the island," he said as he pointed to the north side of the big island.

"I remember a bright light before I faded out. Was that illumination flares fired above the boat?" I asked while searching their faces for a response.

Charlie jumped in and acknowledged he had placed the flares right on target. "Charlie is my name and explosives are my game," he advised with a broad smile on his face.

"Thanks, Charlie," I said sincerely. "It was timely. When they exploded, I didn't know if I was at heaven's gate or seeing the fires of a furnace. I was kind of hoping it was heaven's gate."

I turned to Brett and stated, "You couldn't catch them in the Zodiac could you?"

"No, we couldn't. When we saw you dive into their boat, we pushed off from the island headed your way. We weren't in a position to protect you with small arms fire because the three of you were moving around too much. Plus, it would have been too dangerous to attempt a shot from the Zodiac; we were bouncing across the water. About the same time the driver shot you with the Taser, Charlie fired the flare. That quickly captured their attention. They started their boat and headed out. We dropped Bear and Doc off to attend to you and then gave chase.

Unfortunately, our Zodiac Mark II with a 50 HP Evinrude motor was no match for a Ranger bass fishing boat with who knows how much horsepower. We lost them going up Hurricane Creek."

I was puzzled and told them why. "When those two guys approached me, their engine was hardly running and they needed a tow. Now you tell me their boat is running fine?"

"Doc can answer that question. Can't you Doc," Tonto said, as everyone began laughing. "Doc's a ladies man."

Doc punched Tonto in the shoulder and began to explain. "I'm from Minnesota, the Land of Ten Thousand Lakes. Most everyone had a boat when I grew up and we would take a date out for a boat ride many a time, rather than in the car. In the boat we didn't pretend to be out of gas if we wanted to park with our date. We would manually choke out the engine and the engine would run real rough. After parking with the date for a while, we could fix the engine by manually closing the choke. When I heard their boat tonight, I knew what they were doing. They were choking out their engine to make you believe they were having engine trouble."

"Again, thank you all for your work tonight," I said. "Now Brett, we have a problem. One of the reasons they attacked me is because I now know that those two or their associates are responsible for your dad's death."

Brett was somber as he said, "I know. When I realized they used a Taser on you, I understood how they could incapacitate my dad without any sign of a struggle."

I continued by explaining that his dad's lifejacket and cell phone were in their boat and how the attack on me had started.

"They didn't kill me, so they know they have to come at me again. They know where I live and how to get there by water. That is a good thing because I want them to come after me on my turf rather than theirs. Going to the sheriff for help will do no good, because his department wouldn't believe much of our story if we told them. Will you and your team be around the next couple of days to help?"

"We've pulled duty together in rougher places than this, so what do you think, guys? Thumbs up or thumbs down?" Brett asked. He received thumbs up from each team member and their loyalty to their leader was reflected in the looks on their faces.

Brett then took a moment to discuss their involvement. "Uncle Rick, you know my company has government contracts that I do not want to jeopardize. Therefore, my team will play this out behind the scenes. The less exposure we have to anyone else in this area, the better. Also, for everyone's protection, my guy's nicknames will be all that is required for this operation."

I turned to them all, acknowledged my agreement, and then stated, "Brett, I have one more immediate concern that involves both of us. I am going to call Mary and instruct her to vacate the house immediately and take Gator with her. You need to call your mom and advise her to do the same. They need to do that for their protection and with no argument. Mary will pick your mom up and they can stay at our timeshare in Gatlinburg."

I also added, "We will move the team to my house because I believe they will come after me there. We will be ready for them when they do."

Brett called his mom while I called Mary. I didn't mention to Mary that my head was bandaged. That would have alarmed her even further. Following those calls we turned our attention to how we would move the team to the house.

Brett advised, "We have two vehicles. Our van with our Wells Cargo trailer containing our equipment is parked behind the fire station in Estill Springs. My guys towed the Zodiac down from DC behind our Suburban and it is parked with the Zodiac trailer at Devil's Step. I will assume we won't need the Zodiac in the water because we have your boat and two wave runners, which are all faster than the Zodiac. I'll take Charlie and Tonto with me in the Zodiac. We will trailer it and pick up the van on the way to your house."

"That sounds like a plan to me," I said. "Bear and Doc will go with me and we will see you at the house."

CHAPTER 28

WHEN WE ARRIVED AT the house, Mary and Gator had already left to pick up Sally and head for Gatlinburg. I gave everyone a quick orientation of the house and grounds and where we were located on the lake.

Prior to the building of the dam to form the lake, the Elk River meandered through our portion of Tennessee and was fed by many creeks and streams in the area. When the lake was formed, those creeks and streams (that may have been a few feet wide at their widest point) expanded, in some cases to over several hundred feet wide. Although the creeks and streams became part of the lake, those "extensions of the lake" continued to be referred to as Dry Creek, Rock Creek, Hurricane Creek, etc.

Mary and I live on Rock Creek, which is really a portion of Tims Ford Lake. Rock Creek meets the lake between mile markers twenty-eight and twenty-nine. At that point the old river bed ran west then made a sharp left hand turn to the south. The lake makes the same turn. A bridge on Eastbrook Road crosses the mouth of Rock Creek where it meets the lake. To get to our house, you have to pass through a no wake zone then go under the bridge. A public boat ramp is near the bridge and the no wake zone is posted so that boats will slow to idle speed and not disturb anyone attempting to launch or trailer their boat. As you move up Rock Creek from the bridge, the waterway eventually narrows to a point where it is not navigable by boat. Thus, passing under the bridge is the only way in and out of Rock Creek by water.

After I had oriented Brett's team to their surroundings, we moved to the basement recreation room to map out our strategy and logistical requirements.

"Guys," I said. "I'll start the meeting by outlining our first rule of engagement if, or more likely when, they come after me. It is for our own legal protection. Basically, when possible, we need to minimize any physical harm that comes to those individuals that attack us. We will protect ourselves if attacked, but we must make sure that we will not be viewed as the aggressors by any law enforcement agency. Are there any questions on that?"

Brett chimed in and said, "We have been in similar circumstances in the past and we realize we have to thread the needle between what is legal and illegal. Depending on the circumstances we will face, we brought some items with us that are designed to incapacitate rather than kill or wound. We have twelve-gauge rubber-loaded shotgun shells. These are not steel shells encased in rubber that you may have heard have caused deaths. They are just rubber shells." Brett continued. "If we find ourselves in an enclosed situation, we also brought some Kolokol-1 gas. Kolokol-1 is the same incapacitating agent used by the Russians at that theater under siege in Chechnya. Its use there resulted in some fatalities, unfortunately. Those fatalities were a result of poor training in how to use it. We don't have the same problem. My guys are all trained on how and when it can be used and when it can't."

"That is good to know," I interjected. "Now we need to turn our thoughts toward how we can bring them into the open and corral them. My thought is that they will come to us from the lakeside. They know how to find me from the lake; not by road. Plus, it seems they are more equipped to operate in a water environment. I don't believe they will approach in the daylight. That would be too risky for them. But, we will need to plan for that eventuality and prepare a twenty-four-hour watch schedule. We can rotate shifts of two; one to watch the front approaches and one to watch the lakeside."

Bear volunteered to prepare a roster as soon as our meeting was over.

Brett again took the lead. "We packed Motorola T7450R radios which should handle our communication requirements. They have FCC general mobile radio service (GMRS) frequency ranges which can be used in extended transmit/receive ranges up to twelve miles. We have them equipped with Motorola lapel speaker/microphones which will be helpful in fast moving situations." He continued, "Since the bridge is well within the range limitation of the radios I would station the lakeside lookout under the Eastbrook Road Bridge. To get here by water they have to pass under that bridge. Having someone at the bridge would give us more advanced warning."

"That's a good observation," Charlie added as he turned toward me. "I also noticed that you have electrical power at your dock. In the morning, if you can get me three or four 110-volt smoke detectors, I can place some trip wires on the approaches to the house from the lakeside. I'll modify the smoke detectors in a manner that if they step on the wire, the alarms in them will activate and provide us with another level of advanced warning."

By this time I was wondering what endeavors Charlie wasn't an expert in.

"Charlie, I suppose next you are going to tell me you can convert my television to a radar unit for more early warning," I chuckled.

"He probably could," Tonto said. "Charlie reads and watches so much science fiction, his brain is warped."

Charlie countered. "Tonto, you better be kind to me. Otherwise, I'll tell Rick about your mixed roots! A navy fighter pilot for a father and a marine for a grandfather. I never figured how the army accepted you. But, I guess maybe that was a good thing for us."

"All kidding aside," Brett informed me. "Tonto's nickname is not politically correct. But, he is proud of his Navajo Native American Indian heritage and carries his nickname proudly. His grandfather was a code talker on Guadalcanal, Tarawa, Peleliu, and Iwo Jima in the Pacific during World War II. Love of one's country doesn't get any deeper than what Tonto's grandfather did for his country."

I agreed. Anyone who has seen the movie *Windtalkers* with Nicolas Cage would understand the sacrifices a small group of Navajo's made toward the war effort. Although the movie was titled *Windtakers*, they were officially known as code talkers.

During World War II in the Pacific Theater of Operation, there was a great problem with the Japanese breaking every code the U.S. forces used. Of course, that gave the Japanese key advanced information on where battles were to take place, the strength of the allied units, etc. Something had to be done to combat their code-breaking capability or winning the war in the Pacific would be in jeopardy. The solution was for the marines to use around 400 or so Navajos to communicate war plans and other classified information in their native language, using certain words to represent different frequently used military terms. Code talkers were also used as messengers.

The duty was extremely hazardous because they were constantly required to perform their duties in the forward edges of the battle areas. Their heroics turned the tide of the war in the Pacific in the allies' favor. After the end of the war, high ranking Japanese officers acknowledged that they were never able to break the Marine's code talker code.

Years and years went by after the war before the role of the code talkers was ever revealed. That was because the code was still classified and continued to be used even after the war ended. It was in the early 1990s when the code talkers were first officially recognized for the service they provided to their nation.

I had one last question before we started our preparations. "I believe I now understand how Tonto, Bear, and Doc were nicknamed. But I am still perplexed about how Charlie got his nickname?"

They all laughed and Doc explained. "Charlie married the prettiest little red-haired girl you ever laid your eyes on. He got his nickname from Charlie Brown!"

CHAPTER 29

FOR THE REMAINDER OF the late night hours and throughout the next day, we slept in shifts and prepared for the coming evening hours. We tested radios, reviewed how and to what extent force would be applied to the anticipated interlopers, who would be in what positions, and all the other detail required for an operation of that type. One of the important items discussed was the makeup of teams if we had to divide our small force.

"It didn't look like the Ranger bass boat those two guys were in was outfitted for any type of diving operation. Therefore, we have to assume there are more than two of them and that they have more than one boat. If they bring more than one water craft, we have to be prepared for that eventuality," I advised.

"When we were in the army and engaged in special operations, all of us received training on boats and personal water crafts (PWCs) like your Polaris 150s," Brett advised.

My thoughts reflected back to when I had entered my second childhood and advised Mary that I was going to buy my Harley Davidson motorcycle. She thought it was "a great idea" as long as she could have her Polaris for her and the kids. That is how we came into possession of two Catalina Blue three-passenger Polaris MSX 150 wave runners with all accessories. Mary was always quick to remind me that they were really just like "a motorcycle on the water" for her. Sometimes women don't play fair.

Going back to my discussion with Brett; we decided that if we had to split up and give chase on the water; one sub-team would be comprised of him, Bear, and Doc, and they would have the wave runners. Tonto, Charlie, and I would make up the other sub-team and have the boat.

As we made our preparations that afternoon, we only observed one incident that could have appeared suspicious. Around three o'clock, a pontoon boat with twin Honda four-stroke 225 HP outboard motors and three people aboard passed our dock. Tonto was on lookout at the bridge and indicated the boat seemed to have more than a passing interest in my particular dock.

He advised that they slowed as they approached the dock and all three individuals appeared to be deep in discussion as they looked toward the house. Tonto also observed the pontoon speed up as soon as I walked out onto the back deck of the house. They then continued a couple hundred yards on up Rock Creek before turning around and heading back out under the bridge. He thought they might have been taking pictures of my house, but he wasn't close enough to them to be positive.

What interested me was the size of the outboard motors on the boat. I had never seen a pontoon boat with that much power on the lake before. It also looked vaguely familiar to the boat I had seen trolling on the lake in the vicinity of Verne's Pool on the nights I observed the lights. Even though their actions appeared a little bit out of the ordinary, there was not enough reason for us to attempt to stop them and ask questions.

After supper that evening and a final check of our equipment, we settled in to await what fate might or might not bring our way in the nighttime hours. We only had about four hours to wait!

•CHAPTER 30•

AROUND ELEVEN O'CLOCK BEAR was on watch at the bridge and contacted us. "I'm seeing two boats coming through the no wake zone without any running lights turned on. I'll keep you advised."

In Tennessee, any boat moving on the lake at night must display three lights: a green light on the port (left) front side of the boat, a red light on the starboard (right) side of the boat, and an all-around visible white light at the stern (rear) of the boat. The only excuse for a boat under power not to have their running lights on would be battery failure. On the other hand, if a boat was experiencing an electrical failure, they wouldn't be under power. Two boats under power on the lake late at night without running lights and moving together in the same direction would defy all probability.

I keyed my microphone and said softly, "Heads up, I believe these are the bad guys." In the receiver I heard a series of five "squelch breaks." A squelch break occurs when a transmitter on a radio is keyed but no voice transmission occurs. It can be used by a person in combat like situations to acknowledge that they have received a transmission without having to speak into the radio. By not speaking, they do not risk exposing their position. The series of five squelch breaks I heard told me that the other members of the team had heard my transmission.

As we continued to wait, from our positions near the deck of the house we could see the boats come into view after they passed under the bridge. When they moved nearer and were silhouetted in the moonlight, it became abundantly clear that the lead boat was the Ranger bass fishing boat we had encounter the previous night and following close behind it was the pontoon boat we had seen that afternoon.

They passed by my dock and we noted that there were three individuals in the lead boat and two in the pontoon. For a couple of minutes, I was puzzled as to why they continued past my dock and moved about 300 yards farther up Rock Creek. Then they started to turn back toward the dock and I realized their intent. They had passed by the dock in order to turn the boats around. By doing so they would be headed back toward the bridge when they reached my dock. It was an excellent maneuver and positioned them for a fast getaway by water.

Brett's voice came over the radio. "There are two individuals in the pontoon and Bear's at the bridge. Doc and I will be responsible for those two. Uncle Rick, Tonto, and Charlie, you have the three guys on the boat." Again, a series of five squelch breaks acknowledgements were heard.

The docking of an unlit boat or boats at your dock late at night should be justification for initiating an action against the individuals involved. But our desire was to err on the safe side, so we allowed them to start moving toward the house when they left the boats. One individual stayed with each boat, so only three intruders were moving through the grass toward us. All appeared to be carrying weapons and two had some type of canister in their other hands.

"Wait until they trip the smoke alarms; then use the rubber bullets. If they return fire, use your rifles," I advised over the radio. About that time, the person who had advanced the closest to the house hit a trip wire and the smoke detectors began to emit their shrill alarm.

As the alarms sounded, two things happen simultaneously. I heard the sound of Brett's shotgun discharge and at the same time all three intruders dived to the ground. Because they hit the ground at the same time, I didn't know if any of them had been hit by Brett's rubber bullet shot.

Everything was quiet for a couple of moments. Then we started to receive automatic weapons fire from the two individuals on our left, while at the same time the individual on the right started advancing toward the house with one of the canisters. I attempted a shot at him but my view was partially obstructed by pine trees that grew on the slope to the lake.

When he appeared again he was crawling toward the house and I took my shot. Unfortunately a last-second movement on his part cased my shot to miss him but strike the canister. When the canister was hit, he dropped it, and luckily for him he was a couple feet away from the canister when it exploded into a fireball. Apparently their plan was to firebomb the house.

When the firebomb erupted two things happened.

First, we lost our night vision and our sight was restricted at that critical time. Loss of night vision occurs because at night the pupils of the eyes open farther so a person can see more in the dark. If the pupils of the eyes are suddenly exposed to a bright light, they quickly close farther and restrict vision in the dark.

The second result of the fire bomb eruption was that the hot flames ignited pine needles on the ground and billowing smoke swept across the slope of the hillside leading back to the dock. The smoke obscured our view of the intruders' locations and at that point it was not wise to advance toward them. This gave them the advantage of being able to retreat toward the dock out of our view.

As the pine needles burned down and the smoke dissipated, we saw the three individuals cross the dock and climb into the boats. One was limping noticeably. When we advanced toward the dock we again drew automatic weapons covering fire from the two who had remained on the boats. We returned their fire and at the same time heard the motors on the boats rev and watched them pull away.

My boat and the two wave runners were suspended above the water on their boat lifts. The lifts are comprised of ramps fitted to the top of galvanized tanks that are hinged to the dock. A water craft is driven onto the lift and then an electric blower is turned on to blow air through a rubber hose into the galvanized tank. As the air displaces the water, the tank rises with the water craft perched above it. Lowering the boats involves a reverse process of flooding the tanks so they can sink to a level that allows the water craft to be launched.

We had to launch our boats and wave runners to give chase and I knew time was of the essence. "Cut the hoses leading to the tanks," I commanded over the radio. "That will speed the launching process."

I observed Tonto and Doc draw the Israeli commando carbon steel knives they all carried and immediately cut the rubber hoses. With the hoses cut, the tanks flooded quickly and we launched our boat and wave runners. As we climbed aboard we could see the intruder boats moving under the bridge.

Brett used the radio to advise Bear, who was on lookout at the bridge. "Bear, hold your fire. We are not yet in position to back you up and they have more firepower than you can handle alone. Be prepared. We will pick you up in about one minute. Advise which way they turn when they clear the bridge."

In a couple of moments Bear responded back. "They are splitting up. The pontoon has turned left and is heading up the lake and the Ranger boat turned right heading south."

I couldn't understand why one turned left to follow the old river bed up the lake. Eventually they would run out of water to maneuver in. It appeared that at least the two in the pontoon boat were not familiar with Tims Ford Lake. By turning right, the other three were headed toward the main body of the lake and would have a greater selection of places to hide.

As Bear climbed onto the Polaris Brett was driving, I contacted Brett on the radio. "Brett, stay behind and to the right as you follow them. Don't try to overtake them, but keep herding them to the left as much as possible. They may be in for a surprise sooner than you think."

"Roger that," Brett replied. "I know what you are thinking. If they head upriver, they can't go farther than the bridge at Beth Page Road."

"Right on," I replied.

"I'm not sure we have enough get-up-and-go to keep up with these cowboys," Charlie, who was driving our boat, advised.

I returned my attention to our chase and could see his point. The Ranger boat we were chasing had an inboard motor and was rapidly pulling away from us. My boat was designed more for pleasure boating and was only equipped with a three-year-old 150 HP Johnson engine. Unless they were to by chance run aground in the dark, I saw no way that we could catch them. My concern was further verified when we reached mile marker twenty-three across from Bell Acres and observed them sliding into a left-hand turn at mile marker twenty-two.

When we reached mile marker twenty-two they were no longer in sight. They had either pulled into one of many coves to hide or reached the main body of the lake. With close to 11,000 acres of lake, I conceded that continuing to pursue them would be like trying to find a needle in a haystack. At that point I directed Charlie to turn around and head back so we could help Brett and his crew.

•Chapter 31•

"Brett, we're headed back your way. Can you give me a status report?"

"We've taken some small arms fire. Nothing major. Two holes in our wave runner though. Above the water line. Aunt Mary is not going to be too happy. They've turned under the Estill Springs Bridge and we're heading up river behind them. We are just passing Estill Springs Park now, over."

"Roger that," I replied. "They may attempt to turn right beyond the island into the old strip mine area. Keep them to the left if you can."

"They're taking the channel to the right of the island now," Brett responded.

He then directed Doc, who was in the lead on the other wave runner, to attempt to deny them access to the old strip mine area.

"Heads up Doc," we heard Bear say. "Move under those overhanging trees in front of you. Right now you're silhouetted against the moon."

I could envision what was happening. When you reach the northern tip of the island that sits in the middle of the river, foliage on the right bank no longer exists across the waterway opening to the old strip mine. As he crossed that opening, Doc no longer had trees to his right. Without the trees, his image was highlighted by the moon.

Bear keyed the radio again and we heard distant automatic weapons fire in the background. "Go sidesaddle, Doc—just like I taught you. Put the wave runner between you and them. We're laying down a base of fire to divert their attention."

Brett came back on the radio. "It looks like they thought twice about making the turn to the right. They are continuing upriver with those motors whining. Beth Page Road Bridge is in sight."

"Doc, back it down quickly," Brett added.

Tonto leaned toward me and asked, "Is the river too shallow for their boat beyond Beth Page Road?"

"Worse than that! Very quickly now they are going to realize those two Honda motors aren't powerful enough to propel them over rocks."

"Ouch! That hurts just thinking about it," Tonto replied. "How fast do you think they are moving?"

"If I'm guessing right, they will be going from sixty miles per hour to a dead stop as we speak," I speculated.

About that time Brett came back over the radio. "They've touched down on the rocks. Looks to me like one of the two was thrown out of the boat and the other one is hung up on the front railing and not moving. Doc, does it look the same to you from your vantage point?"

"I see it the same way you're seeing it," Doc replied. "I'll grab the guy floating in the water in his lifejacket if you and Bear can handle the one on the boat."

"Do that," Brett advised. "But be careful. Either one of them could be playing possum."

By then Tonto, Charlie, and I were passing under the Estill Springs Bridge and making our way upriver. The next transmission we heard was from Doc.

"My possum is now road kill. It looks like he took a major blow to his head and his neck is broken. Did yours make it?"

"He's out cold but breathing okay. I think he slid feet first into a rolled up boat cover. It appears the boat cover cushioned the impact to his body," we heard Brett say over the radio. Bear has just discovered something that is strange," Brett continued. "This is the first pontoon boat I've ever seen with a trapdoor in the middle of the deck."

I thought about that for a second and then keyed my microphone. "I do believe that would make it convenient for deploying and retrieving scuba divers without being observed. They weren't trolling for rockfish. It appears they were trolling for divers!"

We needed information and I had an idea.

"Brett, can you see an abandoned white car down near the water on the east bank about 300 meters below the bridge?"

"We have it in sight," he replied.

"Good!" I said excitedly. "We're going to try something, and it may work if the guy that's alive hasn't seen the 1987 movie *The Untouchables* with Kevin Kostner and Sean Connery."

"Doc, can you drag your guy up on shore and lean him up against one side of the car?"

"Will do! I'll get no objection from him," Doc replied.

"Brett, we have you in sight and we'll be there in a minute," I advised. "Haul your guy to the other side of the car. As long as you all have your masks on, don't blindfold him. I want him to see and hear everything that is happening when he wakes up."

By then we were beaching our boat near the abandoned car. This was a spot where teenagers frequently met in the summertime to indulge in a little bit of underage drinking. It was fairly secluded and I wasn't overly concerned about unexpected visitors that late at night.

I directed Charlie and Tonto to gather up some of the empty discarded beer cans and take them out to the wrecked boat that was hung up on the rocks. My intent was to make the scene appear to be an accident caused by drinking, speed, and the driver's unfamiliarity with obstructions on the lake and river. Two of the three conditions in my scenario were true.

I also asked them to make it appear as if only one person was on the boat and to find out if the pontoon had a radio on board. I needed to know if they had had the opportunity to communicate by radio with their buddies prior to the wreck.

I directed Tonto to watch our prisoner and advise me when it appeared he was waking up. Then I pulled Brett and Bear off to the side for a quick conference.

"Bear, I bet you have an acting ability that is just waiting to be discovered. Here is what I need you to do. When our prisoner wakes up, you and I are going to be on the other side of the car, starting to question the dead guy. That may sound strange but remember, the live guy doesn't know his partner is dead." I continued, "When I get no response to my questions to the dead guy, I am going to turn him over to you. I don't expect you to desecrate the body. Still, I want it to appear as if you are killing him because he won't talk. When you finish acting like you're inflicting a great deal of harm to him on that side of the car, toss the dead guy in the water face down. No harm there; that's where he was before Doc pulled him out. Be sure to toss him in where our live friend can see him float by."

Bear responded with a tremendous grin spreading from ear to ear. "The only thing missing from this act will be Sean Connery's accent."

Tonto and Charlie completed their mission and returned from the wreck with good news. They had found no radio equipment or cell phones on board. I then turned to Brett for his guidance.

"Brett. We need to make sure we all wear our ski masks when we are around our captive. Plus, my thinking is the less people we have here, the better. We should also plan for securing this guy when we return to the house. Would it work for you if Tonto and Charlie take the wave runners back to the house and start preparing my cellar under the porch as a temporary holding cell for him?"

"Works for me," Brett replied as he turned to Tonto and Charlie. "Use whatever you need from Uncle Rick's garage. I also believe we have some restraints in the trailer. You can make him a pallet with the cushions from a couple of the lawn chairs. That will keep him off the floor. We'll need a watch schedule also. With restraints, I think only one guard at a time will be needed. Use caution when you approach the house. I don't believe the other guys will double back tonight, yet you never know. If you see anything out of the ordinary, holler for us on the radio."

Brett's last caution to Tonto and Charlie reminded me of one other thing I needed to advise them on.

"My place is secluded by distance and trees from my neighbors and there is no one directly across Rock Creek from our house. Therefore, I don't believe the neighbors would have heard anything earlier and called the sheriff. But if you see any sheriff cars in the vicinity of the house; turn around and come back here.

About five minutes after Tonto and Charlie left, Doc advised us that our captive was regaining consciousness. It was time for Bear and me to take center stage.

•CHAPTER 32•

BEAR AND I MOVED to the side of the abandoned car, where we had placed the dead man. When Doc signaled that the prisoner on the other side of the car was fully awake, I began to question the dead man.

"My friend, rest assured I am not a patient man," I said, directing my voice to the dead man. "I am going to give you one golden opportunity to tell us who you are, why you are here, and who killed my friend. You have exactly one minute to start talking."

I waited one minute and resumed speaking. "I can tell from the smirk on your face that you don't believe I am serious. That is such a bad mistake on your part. Unless you start talking right now, in another minute you won't be able to talk. Because in one minute I am going to turn my back on you and leave your fate to this *man mountain* standing behind me."

I concluded my interview with the dead man by telling him, "Your clock is ticking."

After another minute, of course the dead prisoner didn't respond and I ended my role by saying to Bear, "Animal, tape his mouth so I don't have to listen to his pleas for mercy. Then he is all yours."

I walked in silence to the other side of the car, where our prisoner was sitting wide-eyed on the ground. At that point Bear started his act.

I've read about human acts of cruelty that occurred in ancient and other times. Still, I don't believe any actual or Hollywood-created act of cruelty could be compared to the supposed acts of cruelty Bear, "the animal," inflected on the dead man that night. Without touching him, Bear created the illusion that he was breaking every bone in that man's body.

Throughout it all, our captive's eyes became like saucers. The final straw was when Bear, using only one arm, slowly dragged the dead man to the edge of the river and launched him face down into cold dark water. Now the stage was set to question our hostage.

•CHAPTER 33•

BEFORE ASKING ANY QUESTIONS, I studied the man sitting on the ground before me. He looked to be in his early twenties, slender, with a scar that ran from below his left ear to his cheekbone. My guess was the scar had been inflected by a knife sometime earlier in his life.

His head was shaved bald and he also had some distinguishing pieces of body art that I found interesting. On his head and the knuckles of his right hand were rudimentary tattoos that may have been produced in a jail or prison environment. Perhaps that was where he had picked up his facial scar. His hands were bound behind his back so I used my foot to pull his left hand, which I couldn't see, from behind him. On that hand I also observed tattoos similar to those on his right hand.

The tattoo on the left side of his head was the notorious right-facing German swastika which in World War II came to symbolize the death and destruction brought by the German nation upon the world. Interestingly, the Twisted Cross, as it is known to some, is a religious symbol for many religions, including the Hindu religion. Unfortunately when the Nazis used it on their flag, it became a symbol to fear and is still displayed to this day by most neo-Nazi organizations to demonstrate their support of Nazi teachings.

Using a flashlight I took a closer look at what was written on his fingers and thumbs between the first and second knuckles. On the right hand as I faced him, *third* was spelled out from left to right. On his left hand, *reich* appeared in a similar manner. Apparently, our young hostage had ties to a Nazi, or Aryan Nation, organization.

Although our captive appeared to be visibly upset with the situation he found himself in, he still attempted to stare us down with a defiant glare in his eye. I was silent for a few minutes and backed away while I attempted to determine how we could best extract information from him. Brett joined me and together we reached the decision to use a softer approach toward him, as compared to the hardcore approach I had used in our act with his dead friend.

"In our lives we are sometimes presented with rare opportunities," I said as I walked toward him. "Just as quickly as those life-altering situations appear, they also have a tendency to fade away if we don't seize the moment and act on them. The next couple of minutes will be one of those defining moments in your life. I would suggest you take advantage of it. We need some information from you and we need it tonight. If you are forthcoming and truthful with us, I assure you no harm will come to you. If you don't cooperate; well, you can see what happened to your buddy," I advised as I stared back into his face from behind my ski mask.

"I want a lawyer," he responded with a note of confidence in his voice. "I don't have to tell you a thing!"

"That is a good start. At least you're talking. You are making no sense, but you're talking."

"You made a request and voiced an opinion, so I will address each individually. As to your request, let me ask you this: Do you see a lawyer running around here? Just so we understand each other, this isn't a police station or jail. And furthermore, we are not law enforcement officers. The rules of the game are different out here as compared to what you may have grown used to. Secondly," I continued, "you are entirely correct; you don't have to tell us a thing—just like your friend floating out there didn't have to tell us anything."

I paused and let him absorb that thought.

Playing the good-cop role, Brett jumped into the conversation and suggested, "Let's start with your name. Surely your mother gave you a name."

"Todd," we heard him mumble under his breath.

Brett replied quietly, "See Todd, how easy this is? Todd what?"

"Todd Randell," came his reply.

"Okay, Todd Randell. Now you are making my friend happy," Brett continued as he turned his face in my direction. "Believe me, Todd, there is nothing else in the world right now that is more important to you than keeping my friend happy."

"Have you ever been in jail Todd?" Brett asked.

"No," he replied weakly.

I quickly jumped down to within six inches of his face and shouted. "THAT IS AN OBVIOUS LIE. This isn't baseball, where you are allowed three strikes before you're out. In my game you don't even get nine innings. All you get for the remainder of the night is the chance to tell the truth. Otherwise, it is a short walk down to the water. Now, WERE YOU EVER IN JAIL?"

Todd looked around at Brett and replied. "Several times."

"Where?" I continued.

"Wyoming and North Dakota; once in Colorado. Robbery and assault convictions mostly. One time I stole a car."

"Did you ever kill anyone?" Brett asked.

"Never," Randell responded as sweat popped out on his face.

"Who killed my friend?" I asked in a calm voice.

"I didn't want your friend to die," Randell responded and for the first time we saw a scared look in his eye. "Frank alone approached him that night, used the stun gun on him, and drowned him. I was in the other boat and didn't know Frank was going to kill him." In the dim light he spoke further. "I swear that is the truth. I didn't know it was going to turn out like this."

I had a couple more immediate questions.

"Who's Frank?"

"Frank Snelling, the man your buddy just beat up and threw in the water."

"Okay, Todd. You said you 'didn't know it was going to turn out like this.' What did you mean by that?" I asked.

"They just told me it was going to be a recovery operation and we would be paid well. Will never said anything about killing anyone."

"Let's slow down a minute, my boy," I advised our skinhead friend in a quiet manner. "First of all, you are going to need to tell me who Will is and what he has to do with all this. Then after you tell us about Will, you can enlighten us on what you mean by the 'recovery operation.' But right now we are going to blindfold you and take you to a more secure location. Just don't forget you have no strikes left. If you lie to us we will know it. If you don't know something, *say so*, but don't lie to us. Otherwise, you will be exploring the bottom of the lake without an air tank. Understand?"

"Totally," he answered.

CHAPTER 34

WHEN WE ARRIVED BACK at the house we turned Randell over to Tonto and Charlie for safekeeping and then Brett and I walked out onto the porch to come up with a plan for questioning him. Brett took the lead.

"I think the information we need from Randell falls into two categories. We need organizational information to identify who and what group we are dealing with. We also have to have immediate strategic information so we can plan on how we will handle the other three that are still running loose—that is if there are only three remaining," Brett added. "Then there is the question of what we are going to do with all of them when we are done."

I agreed with Brett's assessment.

"Because you are more familiar with the strategic information you will need in order to brief your team, why don't you lead that portion of the questioning. I am not sure how much he will know about the details and leadership of their organization, but I'll gather whatever I can from him."

We again donned our ski masks and entered the cellar, where Tonto was standing guard over Randell. After releasing Tonto so he could take a break, Brett and I settled in to begin our questioning.

Our captive spoke up first.

"I just want to be away from them and all this mess," he said. "I guess I've done a lot of bad things in my life, but believe me, I've never killed anyone. I've resolved myself to the fact that I will answer your questions no matter what the repercussions to me might be. On the other hand, is there any chance if I help you that I might get some sort of break?"

Continuing to play the bad cop, I answered by telling him the best break he had right then was that he was still alive. Other than that, any other break depended on the extent of his cooperation.

"You mentioned someone named Will," I said. "Was Will with your group tonight and if so, how many others are there here on the lake?

"Will is William Müller," Randell replied. "He lives in North Dakota and isn't here with us. Frank was our team leader. With him dead, there are three others in our group left here on the lake. Craig Hoffman, Owen Bryant, and Calvin Gunderson. Calvin was wounded in his leg when we attacked the dock tonight."

Out of the corner of my eye I saw Brett do a double take when the name Müller was mentioned.

"Tell us what you know about Will Müller," I asked while trying to keep any excitement out of my tone of voice.

"He's the head of the worldwide AFDAG organization."

"I've never heard of AFDAG," I said. "What kind of organization is it?"

Our captive was slow to reply, as if he feared the consequences of responding to the question. "AFDAG stands for Aryans Fighting for the Destruction of the American Government. The AFDAG headquarters is in North Dakota near the Canadian border. You might say it is the Nazi government in exile. They have thousands of members worldwide and, like I said, William Müller is head of the organization."

I thought I knew the answer to the next question but I asked it anyway. "How does Müller plan to finance his grandiose plan to take over America?" I inquired.

Randell looked up and didn't blink. "With the gold and diamonds we were to recover from the farm. He knows they are hidden on the farm. He just doesn't know where. We've been hunting for them and haven't found them yet. According to Will, there is enough down there to buy New York City outright—billions in gold and diamonds."

Brett couldn't stay quiet any longer. He had to jump in with a question.

"Is William Müller related to Helmut Müller?"

"Helmut was William's father," Randell replied.

At that point Brett walked outside and brought Tonto back in to guard Randell. Brett and I then stepped back outside.

"I can't believe what I am hearing," Brett stated excitedly. "The son of Bormann's top aide is alive in our country and is head of a group intent on our destruction. Plus billions of dollars in gold bullion and diamonds are hidden beneath the waters of this lake. We need to bring the FBI on board right away."

"I agree with your assessment, Brett. Nevertheless, we need more information before we can bring the FBI in. We also need to put together a plan of action after we are done questioning Randell. This is amazing information he is telling us. Do you think he is telling us the truth?

Brett was thoughtful for a minute and then replied. "He had no knowledge of what information we had already assembled and what we had already surmised. For that reason, he couldn't fabricate a story around our suspicions—especially a story that so closely aligns itself with facts we have already uncovered. I think he is telling the truth as he knows it."

"Brett, this is an important question that has to do with you personally. If you are convinced he is telling the truth, are you also convinced he wasn't directly involved in the death of your father and that Frank Snelling took that action independent of the others?"

"I am convinced that is what happened," Brett replied solemnly.

As we talked, Charlie walked by us to enter the cellar and relieve Tonto. Charlie had a hot cup of soup in his hand.

"Did the night air get to you, Charlie?" Brett asked as he looked at the cup of soup.

"Nope! It's for that kid. He hasn't eaten in a while."

"Has he talked to you and Tonto much while you've been guarding him?" Brett asked.

"Deep down we think he is a scared young man," Charlie replied. "I was just talking to Bear about him. From what he's told us, he's been on his own most of his life. No family, in and out of trouble since he was eight years old, no guidance when he needed it. He told Tonto he joined that neo-Nazi group because they were like family to him."

"I can't imagine being so starved for a relationship that neo-Nazis would look like family to me," Charlie added.

"Neither can I," Brett added. "Neither can I. On the other hand, our upbringing didn't include having to fight just to exist on the streets since we were eight years old."

We donned our ski masks again and joined Charlie and Todd Randell back in the cellar.

Brett took the lead in the questioning. "Does your team have a place on the lake?"

"They leased a lake place on Little Hurricane Road that has a covered boathouse. We needed the boathouse for cover to load and unload the scuba tanks and other equipment."

"Are there any others in this area besides the three you mentioned earlier?" Brett asked.

"Not that I'm aware of, and I have been here from the start," Randell replied in a more confident tone of voice. He appeared to be less concerned than he was earlier and more willing to cooperate.

"If our associate here brings you a tablet and pencil and removes your blindfold, do you think you could draw a fairly accurate map of the inside of that house?" I asked.

"I'm not much of an artist, but I can draw straight lines. The floor plan is simple—nothing fancy about it."

"Do you by chance know where the heating and air conditioning unit is located at that house," I enquired.

"It's outside on the north side under the bedroom window where I slept. It would rattle and wake me up half the time when it kicked on."

I sent Charlie to get the tablet and Tonto stepped in while we were waiting for Charlie to return. While waiting, Brett directed a curious comment toward our captive.

"From the looks of that scar on the side of your face, you must have had contact with some bad folks in your past."

Randell looked to the floor and spoke in a barely audible voice. "I've had more then my share of standoffs with other gangs, but that is not where I got this," he mumbled as he brought his bound hands to his face and touched the scar.

"When I was six years old I tripped and spilled a beer that my father had sent me to the fridge to get for him. He was so drunk when he beat me he didn't realize he was holding the wrong end of the belt. His belt buckle left this remembrance of him on my face."

A total silence engulfed the room and Tonto turned his back to us. I could see Tonto's shoulders shaking as he tried to keep his emotions in check.

CHAPTER 35

WHEN WE LEFT THE cellar Brett and I poured ourselves a cup of coffee and everyone except for Tonto, who was guarding Randell, sat at the kitchen counter to discuss our next move. Brett was first to express a concern we all felt.

"If we take down the other three guys, my team's involvement would surely be exposed and we can't risk that happening."

"I share your concern," I said. "But with a little bit of ingenuity, our identities could remain a secret," I countered. "Try this scenario on for size. Suppose we capture the other three and they are given the option of being tried as accessories to murder where their conviction is a certainty, or given the option of being tried as terrorists with the hope of a reduced sentence if they turn evidence against Müller and the rest of his people."

"I would bet they would choose to turn against Müller. Yet what they are involved in is not terrorism. Or is it?" Brett asked.

"Hunting for gold and diamonds is not terrorism. But planning to blow up the Tims Ford Dam is," I replied with a smile.

"Uncle Rick, you have a devious mind! Tell us more."

"The props are just about all in place. Those three remaining guys shouldn't know yet the status of Randell or Frank Snelling and right now they must be confused. In the next twenty-four hours we need to take advantage of their confusion. Randell has identified the house they are operating out of. You mentioned earlier that you have a supply of Kolokol-1 gas. Would it be possible to scout out our target during the daylight hours and then after dark tonight inject into their ventilation system enough gas to incapacitate the three of them?" I asked.

Brett advised. "That should be no sweat. The blower on their air conditioning unit could be tripped from the outside in order for the gas to circulate throughout the house. Bear can handle anything mechanical and Doc can handle the Kolokol-1 gas."

Bear turned toward me and asked, "Even after we capture them, which should be no problem, how are you going to convince anyone those guys were going to attempt to destroy the dam?"

"We would need a couple of other items," I replied. "We would need an explosive devise we could plant at their house. The state of Tennessee has a contractor who has been blasting away the rock cliff on the eastbound side of I-24 going up the mountain toward Monteagle. If a couple of you guys could *borrow* some explosives from that contractor, I bet Charlie could improvise a suitable explosive device for our needs."

"Not a problem!" Charlie interjected.

"I didn't think that would be a concern," I said with a smile. "Secondly, I have a couple of maps of the lake that were distributed by TVA months ago. So many were distributed it would be hard to trace them back to a source. If we sanitize them by removing any fingerprints and then draw some arrows on them pointing to the dam, anyone would get the idea that they were interested in the dam. We can plant the maps at their house along with the explosive devise Charlie will build. We will also want to remove anything from that house and the boat that they may have taken from Brett's father. Those items would just lead someone to ask unnecessary questions."

"Is there more evidence we can plant?" Doc asked. It was evident from the look on his face he was excited about the plan.

"I believe I can answer that," Brett said. "The best evidence hopefully will come from the three guys themselves. As Uncle Rick indicated earlier, we will give each of them the opportunity to be tried as a terrorist or to be tried as an accessory to murder. My guess is all three will choose a prison sentence over a possible death sentence and testify accordingly. Plus, if they turn on William Müller and bring about the downfall of his organization, they might have an opportunity to receive a reduced sentence."

Bear then spoke up. "I am still puzzled. If we are successful—and I have no reason to think we would not be—we can't just walk away into the sunset, or technically the sunrise. Who will take ownership of those guys?"

"Good question, Bear. Brett actually answered that question earlier. My plan is to turn the prisoners over to the FBI. I still have high-level contacts with them and I'll make a call to verify their willingness to become involved. Right now I think they will jump at the opportunity."

Charlie turned toward Brett and me with a strained expression on his face. "When you say 'all prisoners' will be turned over to the FBI, does that include the kid down in the cellar?"

"Uncle Rick, before we answer that, would you please excuse yourself for a few minutes and relieve Tonto so I can confer with my whole team."

"Certainly! I'll send Tonto upstairs right away."

Brett's meeting with his team was short and after Tonto again took charge of Randell, I made my way back to the kitchen to a team that was all smiles.

Brett spoke up.

"The answer to Charlie's question is actually simple. Two situations exist. First, many of our government contracts involve the need to infiltrate some very bad groups and gangs. Secondly, the kid downstairs needs a new family. My guys have unanimously agreed they can better provide him with the *parental supervision and direction* he needs. If he agrees, when he leaves here Todd Randell will be the newest member of our team. Now with that issue settled, I need to get my guys moving on their assigned tasks," he said with a wink.

•CHAPTER 36•

THE NEXT DAY CONSISTED of planning and rehearsing for our trip that night to the house on Little Hurricane Road. While Brett and the guys continued to make their plans, the most important task facing me was my early morning call to my old friend and boss, Grant Walters, who was still with the FBI. I called his home to catch him before he left for the office.

"Alice, this is Rick Cheatham and I hope I didn't wake the two of you," I explained when his wife answered.

"Rick, it's good to hear your voice. We miss seeing you and Mary. I told Grant the other day he needed to put out an APB regarding your whereabouts. It's been that long since we have heard from you."

"You make a good point and I am sorry. Perhaps you and Grant could plan a trip to visit Mary and me so we could make up for not staying in touch."

"That would be great," she replied. "Between you and me, he needs to take some time off. He works too hard and I don't want to become a widow at thirty-nine. He tells me I don't look a day over thirty-nine, so I am sticking to that age. That causes some confusion because we have children in their early thirties, but I just say Grant married me young."

"I love a woman that stands by her story," I replied. "Is your roommate up and about?"

"He sure is. Hang on a second while I get him," she said.

I heard Grant pick up the telephone. "I know you wouldn't flirt with my wife while I am still in the house, so this must be something really important," he mentioned with a chuckle. "How is my favorite former agent doing on this fine day?"

"I am doing great, Grant. Mary and I are both doing well. I hate to bother you so early, but I have a situation I need your help on. I also need to be honest with you upfront. Some of your help will involve sticking your neck out and trusting me when you don't have a lot of information to go on."

"That was never a problem when you were working for me and I don't see it as a problem now," he advised. "What's up?"

"It is a long story but we need to get to the bottom line fast. On our lake is a house containing three individuals who are associated with the AFDAG group headquartered out of North Dakota and led by William Müller. Müller is the son of Martin Bormann's former aide-de-camp. AFDAG is intent on the overthrow of our government."

"We've been watching AFDAG for years," Grant interjected. "But we never have had enough to prosecute them on."

"Your luck may change tomorrow. The three guys in the house are part of a team intent on recovery of German World War II gold bullion and diamonds resting at the bottom of Tims Ford Lake. I feel 95 percent confident they have not found that treasure and it is still there. There was one other guy involved down here. He apparently died last night in a boating accident. Alcohol may have been a contributing factor."

"Rick, this is a lot to absorb this early in the morning. Wait a minute while I pour another cup of coffee."

When Grant got back to the telephone I continued. "I will give you an address so you can obtain a search warrant today. Under no circumstances should local law enforcement be advised of your plans. Then, if you can position a SWAT team somewhere in this vicinity by tomorrow morning, I will give you the word when you can raid the house. What you will find is overwhelming evidence that these people were going to plant an explosive charge and blow up the Tims Ford Dam. I am confident their testimony will support that finding. If things go as planned, they should also implicate William Müller and his organization in the scheme, in hopes of receiving a reduced sentence. Don't ask me what their alternative is if they should decide not to cooperate with you. That will be between me and them."

"How will I be sure we have the right ones?" Grant asked.

"They will be duct taped."

"Now that is a sore subject with me," Grant said. "Gray duct tape was one of the last male bastions. Now they have duct tape in a variety of colors. It's just not the same world you and I grew up in."

"I couldn't agree with you more," I lamented to my friend.

"How do you expect us to recover the German treasure if it is down there," Grant inquired. "I've ridden with you on that lake and it covers a lot of acreage. Might be like finding a needle in a haystack trying to find it."

"That is going to require a covert operation on your part," I advised. "I can just about pinpoint where I believe it is. You will need to engage perhaps a team of navy divers and the Army Corp of Engineers to implement the recovery effort. If there is as much down there as I think there is, you may want to give your boss a heads-up regarding that possibility."

"I'll advise the director right away," Grant informed me. "If this call was coming from any other source besides you, he would probably put me in counseling and ask for my early retirement. Fortunately he is familiar with the respect you had in the bureau, so I don't believe he will question my actions."

"I'll head the operation up myself," he added. "How do you want us to maintain contact?"

"I have your cell phone number and will keep you advised on when you can move your team in. In the meantime you will want to advise the navy divers that they will need underwater equipment capable of opening a cistern."

"A cistern!" Grant exclaimed. "What's a cistern?"

"One use might be as a repository for Bormann's treasure," I answered. "Give your bride a hug for me," I said as I hung up the telephone.

•EPILOGUE•

FRANKLIN COUNTY SENTINEL

BOATING ACCIDENT CLAIMS ONE

By Bryan Austin, *Staff Writer*

A boating accident on Tims Ford Lake Saturday night has resulted in the death of an unidentified individual.

According to the Estill Springs Police Department, they responded to a call from a concerned citizen driving to work near dawn who observed an unoccupied pontoon boat sitting idle on the rocks in the waters immediately south of Beth Page Bridge. When police arrived they observed no one on the boat. The Winchester Fire Department Water Rescue Team was summoned to assist at the scene as well as deputies from the Franklin County Sheriff's Department.

According to Chief Roger Sims of the Estill Springs Police Department, his officers immediately initiated a lake search for the missing operator and any passengers that may have been onboard the boat. "It is difficult when there are no eyewitnesses to an accident of this type," Sims commented. "We have to assume the unknown number of occupants did not swim to shore. In this case the search resulted in finding one body floating on the shoreline about one half-mile downstream from the wreck. The victim was still wearing his lifejacket."

According to unnamed sources, the investigation has been hindered because the apparent occupant of the boat was found with no identification. The owner of the boat was located in Jasper, Tennessee, but had reported the boat stolen over six months ago.

The Franklin County Coroner's Office has been asked to investigate due to the suspicious manner in which the death occurred and because alcohol may have been a contributing factor to the accident.

FRANKLIN COUNTY SENTINEL

FBI RAID NETS TERRORIST TEAM

By Jennifer Leigh, *Staff Writer*

An early morning raid by an FBI SWAT team has resulted in the capture of three individuals allegedly intending to blow up the Tims Ford Dam.

Director Grant Walters, who has responsibility for FBI field offices in 16 states including Tennessee, held a news conference today at the Franklin County courthouse to announce the capture of three persons with an admitted association to the group calling themselves for Aryans Fighting for the Destruction of the American Government, or AFDAG. The Aryan organization is headquartered in North Dakota and according to court records is led by an individual named William Müller.

"Today I personally led a SWAT team raid on a residential home in the northern part of Franklin County," Director Walters commented. "The raid was triggered based on confidential information we received earlier that indicated the AFDAG team was intent on destroying the Tims Ford Dam. A half hour after we conducted our raid, an FBI SWAT team also raided the AFDAG headquarters in North Dakota and confiscated all their records. These actions were conducted under guidelines provided in the USA PATRIOT ACT of 2001. From the information we have gathered so far, it appears we have totally disrupted the activities of a large neo-Nazi group intent on the overthrow of our government."

During the news conference, Walters was asked to identify the three men captured. Although he did not identify them, he pointed out that they have been moved to an undisclosed federal location and are undergoing questioning there. He indicated all three were cooperating with investigators.

In an associated turn of events, an FBI spokesman indicated there was a "high likelihood" that the individual who drowned in the Estill Springs boating accident Saturday night may have been associated with the three AFDAG members arrested this morning.

Before the news conference was concluded, Director Walters stated that national security concerns limit the amount of information that can currently be made available. He also was complementary of the cooperation he has received from local law enforcement agencies in "bringing about the downfall of this extremely violent organization."

FRANKLIN COUNTY SENTINEL

ARMY CORP OF ENGINEERS TO PROBE FOR POSSIBLE ENVIRONMENTAL HAZARD

By Noah Ray, *Staff Writer*

Colonel James Lang with the U.S. Army Corp of Engineers office in Chattanooga, Tennessee, announced today that diving operations will commence in the near future in the Maple Bend area of Tims Ford Lake.

"We have been advised that when the Tims Ford Reservoir was developed, one or two fuel oil tanks at a farm on the old Maple Bend Road may not have been drained prior to completion of the dam and flooding of the lake. This is not uncommon and should be no cause for alarm," Colonel Lang continued. "It is a simple matter of locating the tanks, determining if in fact they do contain fuel oil and draining them if they do. Our effort is intended to prevent any contaminates from seeping into the lake."

Colonel Lang explained that divers on loan from the U.S. Navy will perform the dives. He assured everyone at the news conference that there will be minimal disruption to boating traffic and that the recovery effort should be completed within a week's time.

He also indicated that the barge that the diving team plans to use in the operation will be well lit to prevent any nighttime boating accidents. He also advised that "an off-limits buffer zone will be established around the barge for the protection of the divers and the public."

Further questions concerning this Army Corp of Engineers announcement can be directed to their offices in Chattanooga.

FOR IMMEDIATE RELEASE:

News Media Contact: Anna Claire

The White House
Office of Media Affairs

In a surprise move today, President Tyler G. Miller held an unscheduled news conference to introduce what he describes as "a worldwide effort to combat hunger in underdeveloped Nations.

"This program is aggressive and will address a worldwide problem that the American people should not and cannot turn our backs on. Every day there are millions of children in our world who exist without the minimal nutritional requirements to help them grow and become productive members of their society," the President was quoted as saying.

"Be assured this will not be a one-time effort. We have a major source of funding from a previously undisclosed presidential discretionary fund that will finance our goals now and into the future. I have directed my Secretary of the Treasury to prepare a plan to invest those funds over a period of time in government and commercial investments. The income from those investments will ensure that our Child Hunger Abatement Program will continue for years to come."

In his remarks the President also stated that he has directed that the Department of Health and Human Services will have primary responsibility for implementing the program.

"Financing will be provided from investment income controlled by the Secretary of the Treasury, and disbursement of the funds to worldwide faith-based organizations will be under the control of the Secretary of Health and Human Services. This structure will provide a unique form of checks and balances so that all the funds are made available to the hungry children of the world."

When asked how much money was available, the President replied, "There are significant dollars available from the Presidential Discretionary Fund to finance this effort." He went on to indicate that, "no additional tax burden on the American taxpayer will result from this program."

For more information, please contact Anna Claire (annaclaire@whitehouse.gov).

TULLAHOMA STAR TIMES

LOCAL MAN RECEIVES BELATED PURPLE HEART

By Cameron Creed, *Staff Writer*

In a ceremony today attended by area dignitaries, Tony Gladson of Tullahoma was presented with the award of the Purple Heart for a wound he received serving his country in World War II.

The ceremony took place in the base commander's office at Arnold Air Force Base. The award was presented to Gladson by the base commander, Colonel Edward Morgan, acting on behalf of the President of the United States.

In his remarks Colonel Morgan stated, "The Purple Heart is awarded to members of the armed forces of the U.S. who are wounded by an instrument of war in the hands of the enemy. Mr. Gladson received his wound in World War II while serving with the U.S. Army in the European Theater of Operation. Although the exceptional manner in which Mr. Gladson served his country in a time of war has always been recognized, this incident in his military career was somehow overlooked. I am extremely proud today to be in a position to correct that oversight."

Attendees at the award ceremony included a who's who of people within the Coffee and Franklin County community who have known Mr. Gladson for years and are aware of the many contributions of time and monetary donations he has provided to our citizens. Mayor Charles Burns spoke for the people of Tullahoma and said in his remarks, "Everyone in Tullahoma at one time or another, either directly or indirectly, has been positively impacted by Tony Gladson. I am proud to represent those folks today as we acknowledge the sacrifice he made to ensure our freedom."

In his remarks accepting after the award, Mr. Gladson thanked all present, including his family members, for sharing the moment with him. He also told those assembled that he wished his "wife and brother Frankie were alive" to be at his side "on this momentous occasion."

FRANKLIN COUNTY SENTINEL

RETIRED SHERIFF'S DEPUTY PRESENTED WITH TRUMAN PICTURE

By P. Caylor, *Staff Writer*

Hal ("Red") Nelson of Belvidere recently received a pleasant surprise in his mailbox: a letter and photograph from the Truman Presidential Museum and Library in Independence, Missouri. In the picture a much younger Nelson is shown shaking hands with the former President of the United States, Harry S. Truman.

"I was completely amazed when I opened the letter," Nelson explained. "I remember the moment very well but didn't know it had been recorded on film."

Nelson explained how the picture came about. "On June 25, 1951, President Truman flew into Tullahoma in Coffee County to dedicate the Arnold Engineering and Development Center. Although I was a deputy in Franklin County, a lot of law enforcement officers from surrounding counties were detailed to provide security for the President and the others that attended. I remember that Governor Browning, Senator Estes Kefauver, General Hap Arnold's widow, the Secretary of the Air Force, and a whole bunch of others attended."

When asked how he was singled out to shake the President's hand, Nelson replied. "I suppose I was just in the right place at the right time. I was near the front when he finished his speech, and like a good politician, he started shaking everyone's hand. He told me he appreciated all the work we did to provide for his protection. I can tell you, it was a pretty proud moment in my life. And I was proud of him because he and I shared the same political party."

Nelson has had the picture framed and it hangs in the den of the home, which he shares with his sister Rita in the Belvidere community.

A couple of months after the raid on the Little Hurricane Road home, Mary, Gator, and I were relaxing on our back porch enjoying the evening sunset when I received a call from my friend Grant Walters.

"I hope you are calling to tell Mary and me that you and Alice are going to break away and come visit with us."

"I wish that were the case," Grant replied. "If it wasn't for preparation for this AFDAG trial I would be a free man. We'll have to take a rain check. Nevertheless, I will be down your way next Monday and need to know if you and Mary will be around. There is someone that would like to meet with the two of you and we would like you to join us for lunch."

"I'm sure we can handle that. Who are we going to be dining with?"

"I have to avoid answering that question for now, but I'm sure you will find the luncheon well worth your time. Can we meet at the Arnold Lakeside Club out at the Air Force Base at eleven thirty?"

"The time is not a problem, but you might want to meet somewhere else. The Lakeside Club is closed on Mondays," I advised.

"They'll be open," he responded. "Unfortunately, I need to run but will look forward to seeing the two of you Monday."

"Give our love to Alice and we will see you then," I replied as I hung up the telephone.

By the time Monday rolled around our curiosity had reached a fevered pitch but we still had no idea who we were going to be dining with. When we arrived at the Lakeside Club we were met by the manager.

"Welcome Mr. and Mrs. Cheatham. Mr. Walters just called from the base airfield and their plane has just landed. He asked me to apologize for the delay but they should be here shortly. In the meantime, let me show you to the private dining room and bring you a soft drink or glass of wine while you are waiting."

No sooner were we comfortably seated when I heard Grant's voice coming down the hallway. He and another gentleman I recognized then entered our dining room.

"Mary and Rick, it is so good to see both of you again," Grant said as he shook my hand while at the same time giving Mary a hug. "Please meet my boss, FBI Director James Collins."

"It is a pleasure to meet the two of you. And Mary, now I understand why Grant says you are Rick's better half," Director Collins exclaimed with a wide smile on his face.

"Director Collins, the pleasure is ours," Mary said as she shook his hand. "You've come a long way just to have lunch with us."

"My friends call me Jim and I hope your southern hospitality will allow you to do the same. No distance is too far for me to travel to have the opportunity to meet with you and Rick."

From the expression on Mary's face I could tell, in the two short minutes since she had met him, that Jim Collins could do no wrong in her book. Our lunch progressed in that same manner. We discussed our families, the beauty of the Middle Tennessee region, and other subjects that friends might discuss while having lunch together. It wasn't until after dessert had been served that Grant brought up the real reason for their visit.

"Rick, as a formality before we discuss the reason for our visit, I am obligated to remind you that, even though you are retired, you are still bound by the secrecy oath you took as an agent. Mary, we also have to ask you to honor the same oath Rick took. As the two of you will soon realize, this meeting must be off the record. With that said, Jim would like to explain the reason why we flew down here this morning."

Director Collins then retrieved his briefcase from a nearby table and removed two items.

"Rick, I am personally honored to be in your presence today and meet with you, representing our President, Tyler G. Miller," Director Collins began.

"I am sure from viewing news releases that you are one of only a few individuals that can really understand what was found at Verne's Pool. We can also presume that you had a very good idea of the value of the treasures that were located at the bottom of your lake. Yet with that knowledge you did not seek personal gain. You did what was right. You did the honorable thing."

Jim took a sip of water and then continued.

"For the service you have provided to your country and on behalf of the President of the United States, we are here today to present you with the Presidential Medal of Freedom and this letter I have hand-carried to you from the President. He hopes that you understand why this award must remain top secret. Mary, will you assist Grant in placing the Medal of Freedom around your husband's neck?"

With tears in her eyes, Mary stood and completed the ceremony in that quiet dining room.

As I hugged all of them, my thoughts turned back to my friend Johnny. I knew he was beside me in spirit, sharing in acceptance of the award.

Grant then picked up the other package Jim had removed from his briefcase.

"In this box is a very small token presented to you from your friends at the FBI."

I opened the box with the Tiffany and Co. logo. Inside was an ornamental crystal paperweight in the shape of a globe. As I thanked them, I examined the paperweight closer. Imbedded in the crystal was a coin—a pre-war German gold coin.

ABOUT THE AUTHOR

Michael Hart is a retired U. S. Army Reserve officer and corporate manager who resides with his wife in Middle Tennessee at the base of the majestic Cumberland Plateau Mountains.

Printed in the United States
72174LV00005B/166-378

9 781425 949358